D1625935

Snake Vengeance

When Larry Ashfield travels from England to Buzzard's Bend
in Arizona to claim his inheritance, he finds the town's shyster
lawyer, Cliff Makin, has cheated him out of it. The young,
peaceable Englishman is unaccustomed to the rough, tough,
Wild West, and most people in town write him off as a fool and
a coward.

Seemingly lacking the will to fight back, Larry is humiliated
and almost killed . . . until the worm turns with a vengeance.
Death is meted out to his enemies one by one, as Larry
becomes a hell-bent relentless avenger, fighting to recover
what is rightfully his.

Snake Vengeance

Russell James

A Black Horse Western

ROBERT HALE · LONDON

ISBN 0 7090 7469 7

Robert Hale Limited
Clerkenwell House
Clerkenwell Green
London EC1R 0HT

To Clare and Richard

Typeset by
Derek Doyle & Associates, Liverpool.
Printed and bound in Great Britain by
Antony Rowe Limited, Wiltshire

1

THE STOLEN RANCH

Suitcase in hand, Larry Ashfield stepped from the train. He paused, watching the one or two men in cowboy garb and the women in cotton dresses who, like himself, had alighted at Buzzard's Bend; then his gaze moved to the train as it continued on its way. The clanging of its bell sounded mournfully amidst the clouds of steam belching into the shimmering Arizona spring air.

Larry began walking. He was fairly tall, but thin about the shoulders, and twenty-seven years of age. Black, well-brushed hair showed under the grey soft hat he had pushed to the back of his head. His features were regular without being handsome. His pale complexion contrasted sharply with the deeply tanned features of his fellow-passengers, and his grey, well-cut London suit looked out of place here in Arizona. Narrowing his eyes in the glaring sunlight, he caught up with an elderly man in dirt-smoth-

5

ered trousers, and tapped him on the shoulder.

'Excuse me, sir.'

The man gave a slight start, then relaxed as he decided this stranger was harmless. He looked at him quizzically, chewing steadily.

'Where do I find the Double-L ranch?' Larry asked him.

'Double-L?' The old man spat casually and went on chewing. 'I guess it's about three mile yonder – straight that-away.' And he jerked his grey head to one side.

'I suppose I'll have to walk it?'

'Reckon so. Unless you mebbe hire a horse when we get into town. That is,' he added dubiously, 'if you can ride one. You'll be from England, I guess?'

'Yes to both questions,' Larry smiled, as he fell into step alongside the man. 'I'm from London. I'm here to take over my uncle's ranch – the Double-L. You'll probably know of him – Brian Ashfield. Came out here some years ago. Owns a gold mine, too, quite near his ranch.' Larry shrugged his lean shoulders. 'I'm talking as if he were still alive. He died three months back and left everything to me in his will.'

'Yeah, he sure died,' the old man agreed. 'Fell off his horse in front of a steer and it near kicked his brains out. You may be his nephew, son, but you're nothin' like him. He was big and tough – and one of the fastest shooters hereabouts.'

'I've never had cause to be like that,' Larry answered. 'Anyway, thanks – I'll be on my way. I won't follow you into town just for a horse. I don't suppose a three-mile walk will hurt me.'

He began moving away, but the old man's voice called him back.

'Hold on there, son! Who d'you figure you're goin' to meet when you get to the Double-L? Simon Galt's runnin' the spread now. Took possession about a month back.'

'He *what?*' Larry frowned and returned to the old man's side. 'But he *can't* have done! I'm the rightful owner, as my uncle's next of kin.'

'I wouldn't know anythin' about that, son. Just tellin' you how things stand. I reckon you'd mebbe best see Cliff Makin before you go trailin' off to the Double-L. Makin's the lawyer who runs things around here – and I happen to know he was your uncle's legal adviser.'

'Where can I find him?'

'In the main street of town – half a mile or so down the road yonder. His office has a big sign – you can't miss it.'

Larry grunted his thanks, deeply puzzled. In a moment or two he had so quickened his pace that he had left the old man far behind and had arrived at the start of a dusty trail stretching ahead rather like the cart-track to a farm back in England.

Larry mopped his face now and again as the merciless sun continued to beat down. It was hanging just clear of the mountains. In the opposite direction pastureland extended into an expanse of yellow brittle-bush. He winced when he mentally compared its rural primitiveness with the Kensington from which he had come.

He was even more surprised when he saw the town of Buzzard's Bend for the first time as he turned a corner. It reminded him somewhat of an ancient village back home, except that the buildings were of white, sun-blistered wood instead of bricks or cobbles.

The trail he was tramping along ran straight through the centre of the agglomeration of dwellings. They were

7

all shapes and sizes, many of them ramshackle. In front of them ran a boardwalk, overhung by a wooden veranda. In the rutted mass of the 'main street' itself men and women moved, oblivious to buckboards and horses bustling back and forth. The town at least seemed busy enough, even if it was preposterously behind the times compared to London.

At length Larry gained the extreme end of the main street. Wonderingly, he looked about him, dodging the buckboards and teams that occasionally bore down upon him. He realized that he was liable to meet with an accident, so he took to the nearest boardwalk, grateful for the shade the wooden veranda afforded.

Completely preoccupied, he failed to notice the curious looks cast in his direction as townsfolk passed him. Most of the women smiled as though they wanted to be neighbourly, but the men – seasoned veterans of this sunfried dump – winked at each other or spat meaningfully over the boardwalk rail. A white-faced young man with narrow shoulders didn't impress them. The men of Buzzard's Bend lived the hard way, and had no time for anybody who didn't.

Larry was checking out the buildings as he passed them. There was the Lucky Dollar saloon across the street, and next to it a general stores. Elsewhere he spotted a livery stable, a stage halt, an assayer's office, the sheriff's headquarters, the mayor's office – and then, on his own side of the boardwalk, he came suddenly upon a window with gilt letters upon it – CLIFFORD MAKIN, ATTORNEY-AT-LAW. Gauze netting reached half-way up the window, hiding the interior.

The office was small and littered from floor to ceiling

with various documents. Dusty maps hung on the walls. Filing cabinets and a big safe were in one corner. A powerfully built man in shirtsleeves and open waistcoat sat at a roll-top desk, busy with his pen. He turned as Larry entered, swinging round in his swivel chair and putting big hands on the tops of his muscular thighs.

'Howdy, stranger,' he greeted. 'Something I can do for you?'

Larry made no immediate reply. He stood looking rather like a schoolboy before the headmaster – except that there was nothing scholarly about Cliff Makin. He was the kind of man from whom bluff exuded as freely as the perspiration staining his shirt. In a cumbersome kind of way, with his dark eyes and thick and wavy black hair, he was handsome. He was in his early thirties but developed physically by ten more years. At one hip, Larry noticed, sat a pearl-handled .45. Evidently his lawyer's business was liable to sudden challenges from the tougher members of the community.

'I'm Larry Ashfield.' Larry put down his suitcase. 'I suppose you are Mr Makin?'

'Sure I am.' Makin rose, a good six-foot-two, and gripped Larry's hand firmly. 'Glad to know you, son. Mr Ashfield's nephew, presumably?'

Larry frowned at being addressed again as 'son' by a man little more than five years his senior.

'Yes, that's me,' he agreed. 'I've just spoken to a local man who told me somebody called Simon Galt is running the Double-L. That's not right, surely?'

'Well, now I'm afraid it is.' Makin's dark eyes glinted for a moment, and he grinned dubiously. 'Have a seat whilst I explain. Try a cigarette?'

Larry accepted both and waited, considering Makin's heavy features through the blue tobacco haze as he resumed his swivel chair and latched his thumbs in his waistcoat pockets.

'It's this way, son,' he said. 'There was some trouble over the deeds when your uncle died. You may have thought you were entitled to his ranch and gold mine . . .'

'I *know* I am,' Larry replied quietly. 'He wrote and told me he was leaving it to me. I still have the letter.'

'Yeah, mebbe. Anyway, it didn't work out that way legally. You see, this Simon Galt is a big cattleman. Your uncle was in debt to him to the tune of some thousands of dollars. There just wasn't enough in your uncle's account to pay off, so all that could be done was transfer the Double-L to Galt in payment. He accepted the deal and bought in the sole working rights on the gold mine at the same time.'

'Sounds like legal chicanery to me,' Larry said bluntly; and an ugly look crossed the lawyer's face.

'You calling me a crook, son?' he demanded.

'There's certainly something very queer about the ethics of the business. As the next of kin of my uncle, I should have been informed of whatever debts there were. I could either have paid them or given permission for the ranch to be sold up. You've apparently taken the law into your own hands.'

'The whole thing's legal and tied up! Ask the mayor if you've got your doubts. He's the be-all and end-all around here.'

'Evidently,' Larry said, 'Buzzard's Bend has its own queer laws. If this were England I could have you locked up in five minutes for pulling a trick of this sort. It means

10

you've cheated me out of the ranch and the gold mine.'

Cliff Makin stubbed his cigarette down in the brass ashtray and got to his feet, his heavy face menacing. Suddenly he shot down a big hand and yanked Larry from his chair.

'Listen, son,' he breathed, 'don't you go round calling people crooks or you'll end up at the wrong end of a six. My action was legal, and if you don't like it you can go back to England, and stop there. Now get outa here – and quick!'

He released his grip suddenly and Larry stumbled over his suitcase and went sprawling. He lay where he had fallen, his heart beating fiercely. He had been taken completely by surprise. No lawyer in England would ever have reacted in this fashion.

'Mebbe I can help you on your way,' Makin said drily.

Striding forward, he seized Larry by coat collar and seat of his pants, bundled him through the office doorway and then out into the street, tossing his suitcase after him. The door slammed. People went back and forth, unconcerned, as if accustomed to seeing clients thrown out of the lawyer's office.

Slowly Larry got to his feet and dusted himself down. He was looking more puzzled than hurt. Then he turned as a deep voice spoke beside him.

'Anything I can do, son?'

The speaker was a big, red-faced man, silvery hair showing at the sides of his black sombrero. He was dressed in a black suit with a string-tie dangling down his white shirt front. Kindly blue eyes and a generous chin restored some of Larry's confidence.

'I – I don't think so,' Larry replied, raising his suitcase.

11

'I just got involved in an argument.'

'And Makin threw you out? Mebbe he'll do it once too often to somebody. You shouldn't take it, son. Here, take my gun and go right back in there and make him dance a minuet.'

Larry looked blankly at the enormous black-butted .45 the elderly stranger held out. He shook his head slowly.

'No, thanks, sir. I haven't the nerve to try anything like that.'

'You haven't?' The stranger looked surprised. He put the gun back in its holster, a twin to the gun on his opposite hip, then he said, 'Mebbe *I* should go in and tell him a thing or two – Nope, maybe I'd better not. There's a reason I have to be careful about Makin.'

'Why?'

'Well – er – it's sorta private.' The big fellow rubbed his chin, then changed the subject. 'I'm Richard King, of the Bar-6,' and he held out his huge hand warmly.

Larry shook it, introduced himself, and then looked about him. 'Know anywhere in this crazy place where I can get lodgings and not be rooked of everything I've got?'

'Sure thing. You could try Ma Doyle's, across the street there, only I've a better idea. Come back with me to the Bar-6 and make yourself at home. You look to me like the sort of youngster who needs a friend.'

From a man of King's age Larry did not resent the terms 'son' and 'youngster,' but he would have preferred not have heard them.

'I can't put you to all that trouble—' he began.

'No trouble at all. I'm quite well fixed down at the spread. My daughter runs the household, and we have a couple of servants. Just walk along with me. I've a call to

12

make in the general stores, and then I can drive you back in the buckboard.' King was moving with generous strides along the boardwalk as he talked. 'I guess you're a relative of old Brian Ashfield, who died recently? I heard some talk about his having a nephew.'

'Yes, I'm his nephew,' Larry responded. 'I came here to take over the Double-L but Makin's fixed it so that I can't. I've lost a gold mine, too.'

'Cliff Makin is a shyster, son. He's knows every darned trick in the legal book. But I daren't speak out about him too much, because he's liable to become my son-in-law at any time.'

'Your daughter wants to marry him?'

'Not from choice – necessity.' King's face was grim. 'It's sort of involved – and private, like I said. Just wait here a moment.'

Larry waited, pondering events and looking about him as King went into the general store. At length he emerged with his purchase, and then led the way from the boardwalk to a buckboard and team reined to the rails nearby.

Larry tossed his suitcase into the rear section of the buckboard, and then clambered up beside King. The older man jerked the reins and sent the wagon bouncing and rattling along the uneven ruts of the main street. Their journey continued as they reached the extension of the trail beyond the town.

Evening was settling, and the furious heat of the day was abating. Beyond the pastures lay the mountain foothills, covered with red and yellow lichens, peeping out from amidst the purple penstemon. The mountainsides themselves were garbed in junipers, cedars, and oaks. In the opposite direction, facing the mountains, the pasturelands merged into the purple mesa, but before they did so there were acres of golden brittle-bush that was catching the diagonal rays of the sun.

Larry was impressed by the sense of spaciousness and unspoiled nature. It was hard to imagine that people like Cliff Makin flourished in its midst.

'Pretty sight, son, ain't it?' King asked, watching Larry's scrutiny.

'I never saw anything like it in my life,' Larry said frankly. 'I'm city-bred. I suppose you're used to it?'

'You never get used to it entirely. It changes all the time, and is even beautiful in the winter when the snow and rains come. That's my spread over there,' King broke off, nodding into the distance.

Larry saw the ranch clearly as they rounded a bend in the trail. It was fairly large, surrounded by pasture land and corrals wired into neat enclosures. There seemed to be several hundred cattle, and Larry could see the small figures of men going back and forth busily as they roped them in for the night.

At length King had halted the buckboard in the yard outside the ranch house steps. Pausing only to yank his suitcase from the back of the wagon, Larry followed the big rancher up the steps. He found himself in a wide, cool hall.

'Dump your bag,' King said, smiling. 'Come and meet my daughter.'

He led the way into a big, log-walled living-room, the chinks stopped with red clay. The floor was partially covered by mats, and most of the furniture was obviously cedar wood. The fireplace was already smoking before the intense cold of the night shut down. In front of the fire-place was a large skin rug.

14

So much Larry took in before his gaze swung to the girl who had risen from the desk in the far corner of the room. She had apparently been sorting correspondence. Larry noticed that she was of medium height, blonde, with a good-humoured face and rather high cheekbones.

As she came closer Larry noticed that her eyes were blue-grey and extremely frank.

'My daughter, Val,' King introduced. 'This is Larry Ashfield, Val – nephew of our late lamented neighbour, Brian Ashfield of the Double-L.'

'Really?' Val shook hands and smiled. 'Well, this is quite a pleasurable surprise, Mr Ashfield. You'll be taking over the Double-L, I suppose?'

'I wish it were that easy,' Larry sighed. 'As I've been telling your father, I'm afraid I've been cheated out of my inheritance.'

'Gypped,' King said grimly. 'And by that no-account Cliff Makin . . .'

He detailed the circumstances in which he had met Larry, and the girl frowned.

'I'm sorry to hear of this, Mr Ashfield,' she said, 'though, knowing Cliff as I do, it doesn't come as much of a surprise.'

'I believe you're engaged to him?'

Val King turned away slightly. 'Not yet. I haven't committed myself.'

'You'll be wanting a meal, son,' King interrupted, 'and then a rest. You've had a long journey and a tough disappointment at the end of it. Come with me, and I'll show you where you can freshen up. After we've had supper, maybe you'd care to tell us a thing or two about yourself.'

2

POKER MAGIC

By the time supper was over – prepared and served by two extremely uncommunicative Indians, an Aztec and his squaw, the night had fully come. Within the big ranch living-room, however, twin oil-lamps were burning brightly. In the immense grate two logs crackled warmly. To Larry, seated opposite the girl and her father on the other side of the fire, it seemed queer that such blazing heat could change to cold within a few hours.

'Naturally,' he said, 'I cannot stay here, kind though you have been. Since I've been cheated out of everything, there's no point in my staying in the district.'

Richard King lighted his pipe slowly. His daughter studied Larry's regular features, frowning slightly to herself.

'You mean you're running out?' she asked bluntly.

'I've no choice, Miss King. I'm no lawyer. I can't fight Makin's legal knowledge.'

'Around here one doesn't need legal knowledge to get one's rights – or anyways a *man* doesn't,' the girl said, and there was a sting of contempt in her emphasis. 'Nobody would gyp *me* out of a prosperous ranch and a gold mine

16

without a mighty big struggle.'

'I'm not the kind of man who can take the law into his own hands,' Larry said, looking moodily into the fire. 'In England, we just don't behave like that.'

'I don't believe it,' King declared. 'It's just a matter of not being sure of your surroundings. Stick around for a few weeks, get acquainted with the habits of the men who run Buzzard's Bend – then make up your mind.'

'It's made up,' Larry responded, shrugging. 'If we were in London, I could hand the matter over to the police to deal with. Out here there's no real equivalent.' He glanced across at the big rancher. 'I'm discounting the mayor and sheriff, since you've told me they're in cahoots with Makin.'

'You've got two fists and a fair-sized frame!' Val exclaimed. 'What more do you want?'

'I simply don't have the experience to use them. In London we just aren't used to fighting amongst ourselves, which you seem to take for granted here in the West.'

'Around here,' King said, 'a yellow streak means gold, son. That's what I'm going to go right on thinking. As for you – well, I think you should stay and get acquainted with the way we do things. What do you do for a living?'

Larry smiled rather ashamedly. 'I'm a professional magician. As an amateur I did quite well in charity concerts, so I went on the halls as a professional afterwards. Nothing big. Card-tricks, water to wine, mysteriously dissolving knots in ropes, and so on.'

'Sounds mighty peaceful,' Val remarked drily.

'It is. Once you've mastered them, the tricks work themselves. When I heard of this inheritance I packed up everything, gathered together what money I possessed, and came right away. Now all I can do is go back.'

The awkward silence was broken by a thunderous pounding on the outer door of the ranch. Val gave her father a significant glance.

'That'll be Cliff,' she said, and rose to her feet.

'Maybe I'd better go, too?' Larry rose to his feet. 'He won't be exactly pleased when he sees me here.'

'Then he can be the other thing,' Val answered briefly. 'Sit down, Mr Ashfield!'

At that moment the living-room door opened and Cliff Makin appeared. Since Larry had seen him he had dressed in his best attire – a black suit with a neat tie, revealing an expanse of shirt front. His wavy black hair was gleaming with oil and a razor had obviously travelled closely over his heavy features.

With hardly a glance around him he strode over to Val, seized her, and delivered a kiss. Larry saw her slim hands clench momentarily at her sides.

'Hello, Cliff,' she said indifferently.

'What kind of welcome is that?' he demanded. 'One would think I . . .'

He stopped dead, catching sight of Larry in the dim light.

'Cliff Makin – Larry Ashfield,' King said quietly.

'I know who he is,' Makin snapped. 'I threw this kid outa my office this afternoon. What the hell are you doing here?' he demanded, striding over to where Larry now stood by the fireplace.

'I'm a guest,' Larry explained, shrugging.

'Well, I don't like it – and what's more I won't have it. Get him out of here, King, and pronto.'

King hesitated, his powerful mouth setting. Val gave a

18

desperate glance from one man to the other.

'Don't forget I've as much say in what goes on on this spread as you have,' Makin sneered. 'I don't like the smell of this critter from England.'

'Cliff, for heaven's sake!' Val cried. 'Mr Ashfield has nowhere else to go and—'

'That's rubbish, Val!' Makin swung round on her. 'There are plenty of places where a man can stop in Buzzard's Bend without coming here. You don't suppose I'm letting him stop here with you around, do you? You're young and mighty attractive otherwise I wouldn't be bothering with you myself. I'm assuming that this British kid has some manhood in him, so I'm not taking chances—'

Makin stopped, his cheek smarting from the vicious blow Val gave it with the flat of her hand.

'You get out of here, Cliff, with your low-down suggestions,' she said briefly, her angry eyes pinning him.

'OK, mebbe I did speak a bit out of line,' Makin admitted. 'But this guy gets in my hair. Doesn't even act like a man even though he's shaped like one. Anyways, I'm expecting you to throw him out, if you know what's good for you. Now, Val, how's about riding into town as usual? I've a table for us at the Lucky Dollar.'

'You can keep it.' Val set her mouth. 'I'm not coming.'

'Is that because you like it better at home now you've got company?'

'You'd better go, Cliff,' King said coldly.

Makin hesitated and then grinned sourly. 'Better take it easy when you start ordering me about, King. May not work out the way you think. I'll go, since I'm wasting my time tonight. But I'll be back tomorrow, Val, to keep my usual evening date. And when I come I'll expect to find

19

this louse half-way back to England.'

He snatched up his hat, went out, and slammed the door. There was silence for a moment, then Val relaxed a little and sank back on her chair.

'And that is the – the *pig* I have to marry!' she whispered at length.

'Take it easy, Val,' her father murmured, with an uneasy glance towards Larry.

'Why should I?' Val cried, springing up again. 'Every other person in town knows why I'm going to marry Cliff What is there to stop Mr Ashfield knowing?'

'I don't want to pry into your business,' Larry said uncomfortably.

Val turned to him. 'I think you ought to know, Mr Ashfield, in case you have a wrong impression. I'm going to marry Cliff Makin to pay off a gambling debt!'

'Val, for heaven's sake . . .' Her father raised his hands in protest.

'No Dad, I'm the pawn in the whole thing, so I'm entitled to say what I think. You ought to know, Mr Ashfield,' she continued, returning her attention to him, 'that my father recently gambled away this ranch and all it contains in a poker game. He was playing with Makin, of course. That means Makin owns this place. We go on living in it and carry on our cattle business only through his generosity! That's what makes me so – so *sick*! If I marry him he will legally cancel the debt and we can go on with our business – or at any rate Father can, since I suppose Cliff would keep me. But if I refuse we lose everything. We're only going on now because Cliff fully believes I'll become engaged to him before long. We can't sell out and go elsewhere. Cliff Makin has us – and me in particular – hog-tied.'

'I'd made a good cattle deal,' King explained bitterly, staring into the fire. 'I'd plenty of money with me – but too much celebration liquor under my belt, I guess. At that time I didn't know the kind of rat Makin really is. He'd paid attention to Val, so I thought he was a friend. Then I got into that poker game. I was so dad-blamed fuddled with whiskey I couldn't even think straight . . .'

'And there's nobody to whom you can appeal?' Larry asked, after a pause.

'Against a gambling debt contracted before dozens of witnesses?' King asked. 'No! Makin has the deeds and he's performed the legal transfer of the property to himself. Even if there were a loophole, the sheriff wouldn't do anything. He – and the mayor too – are in cahoots with Makin. I tell you, son, these days the whole of Buzzard's Bend is rotten from the dust up.'

'So your daughter has to take the blame?' Larry asked quietly. He sat down again and reflected. Val and her father looked at Larry as though they expected some kind of miracle to happen.

'Killing him is out,' King said at last. 'I wouldn't think twice, but the rap's too tough if I should be caught. With a fixed sheriff and mayor I wouldn't stand a chance.'

Val gave her father a reproachful glance. It was clear she didn't approve of plain murder under any circumstances.

'There may be another way – one that doesn't involve getting tough with guns,' Larry said, thinking. 'We could win this ranch back from him – once again by gambling. He'd be forced to hand over the deeds, if they were the stake played for. The witnesses round the table would see to that. Even if the sheriff and mayor are crooked, I'm sure

21

the rank and file are not.'

'No – most of them are square shooters,' King admitted. 'But I wouldn't like to take the risk of gambling like that again. If I lost I'd be worse off than ever.'

'I was thinking of myself,' Larry said.

'Then I hope you can play poker well, son,' King said dubiously. 'Makin is one of the best players in town – even playing straight. When he does it the crooked way he's dynamite.'

Larry smiled faintly. 'I know the rudiments of poker enough to get by. My strong suit is magic. Hand me a pack of cards,' he requested.

'It's a "deck" out here.' Val smiled, and went over to the bureau. Returning, she put a practically new pack into Larry's hand.

He shuffled them casually for a moment, then the cards began to do things which made Val and her father watch in fascination. They leapt from hand to hand in a mist, divided and sub-divided, threw out all their aces at will, transferred their kings to the bottom and the queens to the top, until with a final flourish Harry fanned the cards down on the table top and every one was in its correct suit from ace to king.

'Why – that's marvellous!' Val cried, clapping her hands.

'Useful anyway,' Larry responded with a modest grin. 'I can do it with any pack – I mean deck; and since I'll be given a new one when I play poker it shouldn't make much difference. If I win I can get everything back that you have lost. If I fail . . .' He debated this for a moment. 'Well, if I fail it can't make matters worse for you: only for me. Yes, I'll take the chance.'

'And the boy says he hasn't got courage!' King exclaimed, with a glance at his daughter.

'This isn't the sort of courage I want,' Larry sighed. 'I want the kind of courage you Westerners have, where I can stand up to a man and hand him back everything he gives out. In the meantime I'll have to try other avenues. Do you suppose I have time to go to the Lucky Dollar tonight and start a game?'

'Sure,' King said. 'Things don't warm up in that place until around ten-thirty, and it's only quarter before nine as yet. I'll come with you.'

'So will I,' Val said eagerly, and fled from the room to change for the outdoors.

'I'll get the buckboard ready,' her father said, and followed her.

Larry half-smiled to himself and picked up the cards slowly. Each in their suits, he put them back into their carton . . . .

The Lucky Dollar was at the height of its evening's business when the trio entered through the batwings. Larry coughed for a moment at the foul air that smote him after the sweetness of the night; then he recovered himself and looked about him.

Curious glances were cast at him by the men and women at the tables and around the bar. A young, pale-faced man in a 'civilized' grey suit and soft hat was something new in this den of cowpunchers, cattlemen, half-castes, and passers-through. Since Richard King was a frequent visitor, scant attention was paid to him, but it did seem curious for his daughter to be present, looking highly delectable in her silk shirt, fancy-edged mackinaw, and black riding-pants.

'You drink?' King asked Larry suddenly.

'I can take whiskey, even though I'm not keen,' Larry responded. 'I realize I can hardly walk into a place like this and order milk.'

'Then we'll go to the bar,' King decided, and led the way to it.

The stares followed them. The place buzzed with conversation, the rattle of chips and faro wheels, the clink of glasses and bottles, and the tin-panny rattle of a 'three-piece orchestra' on a distant rostrum. The whole place was garish, from the gilded back-bar mirrors to the ornate pillars supporting the wooden roof, from which hung clusters of gleaming oil-lamps.

At the bar, King gave the order, Val taking a soft drink. Then they stood and looked about them. One or two of the punchers nearby winked at one another and left it at that. Larry, leaning against the counter, suddenly came alert as he caught sight of Cliff Makin heading towards him, his twin guns showing at his hips as his black coat fell apart.

'Well!' he exclaimed, coming level. 'So you decided to keep your date after all, Val? And brought your pop and the lodger with you, huh? Frankly, I don't appreciate the passengers!'

'I'm not keeping a date with you,' Val responded levelly. 'It's Mr Ashfield who's doing that.'

'Huh?' The lawyer looked at Larry blankly. 'What the tarnation would a little runt like you want with *me*? Or don't you know when you've had enough?'

Larry took a grip of himself and straightened.

'You call yourself a good poker-player, Mr Makin. Are

24

you prepared to play a game with me?'

Makin's dark eyes opened wide; then suddenly he exploded with merriment. He laughed so hard the gold in his back teeth showed transiently.

'Sweet hell, that's a good one!' he gasped at last. 'Will *I* play poker with *you*! Why, you cheap out-town tenderfoot, I'll wipe the floor with you before you know what you're doing. Run on home, sonny, and don't waste your time.'

Makin turned away in contempt, then stopped as Larry's quiet voice reached him.

'I'm serious, Mr Makin. I'm challenging you to play for the Bar-6 ranch.'

Makin turned back again, genuinely baffled.

'Let's get this straight,' he said. 'Are you actually telling me that you want to try and win the Bar-6 back from me?'

'That's it.'

'You're loco,' Makin decided; then his eyes narrowed suspiciously. 'Why this crazy notion to try and get the Bar-6? So you can give it to Val here? That it?'

'Never mind the reasons,' King snapped. 'You're being made a straightforward challenge, as all the rest of the folks in this room can verify. You won the Bar-6 from me; but that doesn't say it can't be won back again.'

'Unless I don't choose to let it be the stake,' Makin responded, thinking. 'And what about *your* stake, Ashfield? What's in it for me if I win? You've got nothing I want – and you probably ain't got the equivalent in cash, either.'

'I've got my claim to the Double-L,' Larry said. 'Not to mention the gold mine that goes with it. You and I both know that it's rightfully mine. If I was to hire a big-time lawyer from Austin, and show him my uncle's letter to me, he'd start investigating your activities. You may be a big fish around here, but I doubt your crooked practices could stand up to intense outside legal scrutiny. If I lost to you I'd be prepared to surrender the letter to you and sign a deed giving up my claim to the Double-L completely. You can draft the deed yourself and I'd sign it.' Larry paused, watching Makin's expression. He could see he was wavering.

'There's your stake, Makin. A ranch for a ranch.'

Makin still hesitated. 'I rather like having the Bar-6. Makes King do as I tell him. If I lose it, that power's gone. And his daughter with it.'

'You can leave me out of it,' Val said briefly. 'I want nothing more to do with you, Cliff, after your remarks tonight. Nothing will alter that, whether you own the Bar-6 or not.'

Makin grinned. 'I don't give in that easily, Val, when I want something – and I sure want you. All right, son,' he added, plainly amused, 'I'll play you.'

Larry nodded and followed Makin through the crowded room to a vacant table. The lawyer sat down, cuffed up his hat, then lighted a cheroot. Larry sat down, too, half-smiling to himself, his pale face very intent and thoughtful. King and Val stood behind him. An interested knot of spectators was already beginning to gather.

'Drink?' Makin asked. 'Or would that blow those little-boy guts of yours apart?'

'Whiskey,' Larry said quietly.

Makin nodded and waved his big arm. 'Hey, Curly, some whiskey over here – and bring the bottle. And a new deck of cards.'

'Coming right up,' a waiter responded; in the space of

26

perhaps three minutes Makin had the playing-cards beside him in their new carton, and a bottle of whiskey and two glasses at his elbow. He filled the glasses, pushed one across, then eyed Larry fixedly through the haze from his cheroot.

'Toss for dealer,' he said, and Larry nodded.

A coin spun in the air from Makin's hand and landed with a clink on the table. He called and clamped his palm over it, then withdrew his hand.

'You deal,' Larry said, and put down his half-empty whiskey glass.

The 'orchestra' on the rostrum had stopped its noise. The activity at the other gaming-tables had ceased. There was a curious breathless quietness in the big room. The prospect of Buzzard's Bend's most accomplished gambler playing a civilized tenderfoot promised some fireworks – for the tenderfoot.

Makin tore the card wrappings and then sliced the cards through his hands quickly. Larry did not move a muscle. Behind him, King and Val glanced at one another. Then Makin dealt five cards to Larry and five to himself. The remaining cards he put on the table before him and squared them up, face down.

'The ante's the Bar-6,' he said, 'and your alleged claim to the Double-L. That's all we need to know. All right, let's get started.'

Larry said nothing. He was examining his cards. Makin studied his own hand, peered through narrowed eyes at his opponent for a moment, and then seemed to be trying to make his mind up.

'Two,' Larry said, and started the game.

Makin began playing cautiously at first, apparently to

make sure of the type of man he was dealing with; then gradually he took greater chances. He threw away possible tricks and instead took cards from the undealt pack. After a while a hard grin came to his features.

'Triplets,' he said, throwing them down.

'A straight,' Larry countered, announcing a trick higher, and he fanned his cards on to the table.

'That lets you out, son,' King said. 'You've won the game. What about it, Makin?'

Makin chewed his cheroot to the corner of his mouth. He seemed about to say something, but Larry cut him short.

'We're not giving the onlookers a run for their money, Mr Makin. I've won back the Bar-6, and I'm holding you to it, with these folks as witnesses. But I'm prepared to go on playing to give you a chance of beating me. Only sportsmanlike, I guess.'

'For Pete's sake, don't be a dad-blamed fool!' King cried. 'You've got all you came for.'

'Maybe, but it's too soon to quit. I'll raise the ante, Mr Makin. Five thousand dollars *and* the Bar-6. We don't need chips to that value: that's the stake, and these folks are witnesses.'

'Have you got five thousand dollars if you lose?' Makin snapped.

Larry smiled. 'I've got that and more in a bank at Austin. I sold up my property in London before moving out here.' It was a bluff, he'd lived in rented accommodation, but Makin wasn't to know that. 'Anyway, I shan't lose. Hand me the cards. My turn to deal.'

Makin pushed them over, then he watched with startled eyes as they whirled and gyrated like leaves in Larry's prac-

28

tised hands. One or two of the onlookers gasped and looked at one another. Such fancy shuffling had never been seen in the saloon before.

'Right,' Larry said at last. He dealt out five cards apiece, putting the remainder face down. 'This is it, Mr Makin. You or I are going to finish up the richer by the Bar-6 and five thousand dollars. Your call.'

There was a long pause, Makin biting hard on his cheroot as he studied his cards; then he began to smile. Eventually he laid his cards down slowly, and his smile widened.

'Fours!' he declared in triumph. 'Beat that if you can!'

Larry nodded, and laid down all his own five cards, a sequence in spades.

'Royal straight flush,' he said drily. 'There's no hand higher than that, Mr Makin.'

Twice in the history of the Lucky Dollar gamblers had pulled off the near-impossible top trick in poker – and this was the third time. But for a civilized tenderfoot to have done it was something close to a miracle. For quite five seconds Makin stared fixedly, then he leapt to his feet and overturned the table in his fury.

'You blasted, two-timing lily-white!' he yelled. 'You fixed the cards—'

Larry backed away, overturned whiskey pouring down his trousers. Then King sprang forward and seized Makin's powerful arms, holding him back.

'Lay off him, Makin,' he snapped. 'That was a straight trick – and you know it.'

The lawyer breathed hard, fighting for control. Then, his swarthy face dark with rage, he swung to a nearby waiter.

'Hey, Curly,' he snapped. 'Come here and pick up these

cards. Count out fifty-two of them on the table and let's see if they're straight.'

'Sure thing, Mr Makin.'

The waiter did exactly as ordered, then he righted the table and counted out the fifty-two cards, each in their suits. At the finish there was no doubt. The pack was genuine enough.

'Well?' Larry asked quietly, holding his soaking trouser leg. 'Satisfied, Mr Makin? I'll trouble you for five thousand dollars and a deed transfer for the Bar-6.'

'In the morning,' Makin growled, making to turn away – but the barrier of people blocked his path.

'We want it now,' King stated flatly. 'These folks here will see that we get it.'

'Yeah, sure,' somebody murmured.

'Better do it, Cliff. You got yourself hogtied.'

'All right,' Makin replied, realizing he was cornered. 'I'll have to go along to my office.'

'I'll come with you,' King said, yanking out his gun just in case. 'Start walking.'

Makin pushed his way through the crowd. As he did so he caught a grim look from the paunchy Sheriff Crawford, who had been watching the proceedings; but on this occasion, unless he wanted running clean out of office, there was nothing the ferret-eyed sheriff could do. Makin had cut his own throat.

Larry turned a little as Val put a gentle hand on his arm.

'Thanks, Larry,' she said, her voice low. 'If you don't mind my calling you that?'

'Sounds better than mister,' he responded, smiling. 'Glad I could help you. That lets you out with Makin, doesn't it?'

'Definitely. In any case I'd have had nothing to do with him henceforth, though – as I told you – you certainly know how to play poker.'

'Perhaps,' Larry murmured, his voice low. 'The hardest part was shuffling my straight flush so it began at the sixth card from the top of the deal. Nimble fingers can be useful sometimes.'

He did not say any more, for the people were crowding in on him to shake hands and congratulate him. Most of the men and women seemed pleased that Makin, the self-assured gambler, had been smashed flat on his face for once. Larry took all the eulogies in his usual undemonstrative fashion; then he looked up as Makin reappeared, a deed and some high-denomination dollar bills in his hands, King with his gun right behind him.

'There it is,' Makin snapped, flinging the transfer deed on the table. 'Made out to you, Ashfield. I fixed that in my office. You'll find it's legal enough. And here's the five thousand dollars.'

Larry picked up the deed and the money, and stuffed them in his pockets.

'Thanks,' he said. 'All I've got to do now is to get this deed transferred again to Mr King – through a lawyer who can be trusted, which certainly doesn't mean anybody in this town. Which means, Mr Makin, that your presence at the Bar-6 will not be welcome in future.'

'Don't give me orders,' Makin breathed. 'I'll go where I like – and if you think I've finished with you, Val, you're crazy.'

'If you turn up again now that you no longer have control over the spread, I'll have you thrown out,' King said grimly, holstering his gun. Then he glanced at Val and

Larry. 'Let's be going,' he added, and led the way from the table.

Makin watched them move, and then he glanced at some of the cowpunchers around him and nodded. Instantly things began to happen. King found himself suddenly seized from behind, and, powerful man though he was, he was impelled through the batwings at top speed and then carried along the street, helpless in the grip of four men.

Larry, for his part, received a blow in the jaw that sent him staggering against the wall of the saloon. A second one nearly lifted him from his feet. Half-senseless, he was picked up between two of the men and carried in the wake of King down the street. Val, unable to do anything about the matter, stooped quickly and picked up the deeds and money that had fallen from Larry's coat in his sudden collapse. She was about to push them in the inside pocket of her mackinaw when Makin's hand closed over her wrist.

'Thanks, Val, I'll take those,' he said briefly. 'You don't suppose I'm going to let Larry Ashfield get away with them, do you?'

Val hesitated, then she found the money and deeds snatched from her fingers.

'And I meant what I said about you and me,' Makin added roughly, his free arm crushing about her slim waist. Val gave a gasp and squirmed fiercely, but it did not save her from two revoltingly long kisses. Makin would probably have tried a third time, only her foot suddenly lashed out and kicked him hard on the shin. He gave a gasp as the point of the hard riding-boot bit into his flesh. Val went further, and kicked his other leg – then she shoved with all the power of her strong young arms.

Makin stumbled backwards slightly, giving a yell as he saw Val whirling up an empty bottle from the table at her side. He was not quick enough to stop her bringing it down on his head with stinging force. His hat saved him from cuts but his senses reeled under the impact for a moment.

Dishevelled and breathing hard, Val snatched the deeds and money still in Makin's right hand and then dived for the batwings. Two of Makin's cohorts tried to stop her but she dodged beneath their outflung arms and hurried outside. At the sight of four of Makin's men returning up the main street, she felt quickly at her shoulder holster and pulled out a .32 automatic, levelling it.

'Keep away from me,' she ordered, circling the men carefully as they hesitated. 'I'll shoot if you try coming nearer.'

They didn't. They had sense enough to know that the daughter of Richard King must be a first-class markswoman – as indeed she was. So she got past them safely and then halted again at the vision of her father and Larry rising from the horse-trough and dripping water from head to foot.

'What in— What happened?' she gasped in alarm, reaching them.

'Oh, just a little spite on Makin's part,' her father responded, wading out of the water to the dusty street. 'You OK, Larry?'

'Good enough,' Larry assented, water dripping from his hair. 'I guess I wasn't much use when it came to fighting back. I'm just not used to it. I'm sorry.'

'So am I,' King growled. 'If you'd have had the guts we could have plastered the walls with those guys.' He looked

33

his surprise as Val suddenly started to laugh.

'Sorry,' she apologized, 'only you both look so funny! Anyway, Larry, you got the ranch back and five thousand dollars, too – even if I did have a fight to retain it.'

'Fight?' Larry repeated, surprised. 'Do you mean these low-downs actually fight girls, too?'

'Not quite that.' Val set her jaw. 'Cliff tried to pin me down for his own gratification. He got in a couple of kisses, then I kicked the tar out of him and ran for it. He'd planned to get the deeds and money and put things back where they started. He failed, though, and he certainly won't get another chance. I can still feel those filthy kisses of his.'

'I've a mind to go right back in there and square things up for that,' King breathed. 'He's got nothing on me any more, so. . . .'

Val shrugged. 'I dealt with it, Dad: not your job.'

She gave Larry a meaning look, but he was not looking at her. He was squeezing water out of the hem of his coat.

'We'd better get our horses and hit the trail for home,' King said. 'Soaked like this, we might catch cold in the night air. Let's be moving.'

They returned to their horses without molestation, and then began the ride back home. Evidently Makin had decided to call off the dogs for the moment. In fact, having failed in the initial attempt when the deeds were in his grasp, he probably realized he would never get the chance again. It was doubtful if the ordinary townsfolk – who had been taken by surprise when Makin's supporters had acted – would permit a second similar attempt.

'Do you suppose,' Larry asked thoughtfully, as they rode along, 'that I could handle difficult situations better if I had a good knowledge of gun-play? I mean, would it help me to make up the deficiency in my physical toughness?'

'Might,' King said. 'Why?'

'I've been thinking. I ought to make Makin apologize for the way he treated you tonight, Val.'

'I can do without that,' she replied. 'I don't want you risking your neck trying to shoot it out with Makin.'

'That's not quite the point. . . .' Larry rode on steadily for a while. 'I don't want to stay low down in your estimation, Val. I know exactly what you are thinking about me – and you are right. Somehow I've got to change your opinion.'

'I'm willing to help you learn our ways,' she responded. 'I can't give you courage, of course, but I can show you all the tricks as far as guns are concerned. Dad's shown me every one of them, so I can pass it on. But, Larry, don't get the idea that I think badly of you. After the way you played tonight—'

'That was nothing,' Larry interrupted. 'Just sleight of hand. What I have to do is be able to settle Makin completely if he continues to bother you.'

'We'll fix you up somehow,' King declared. 'Keep on staying with us, and in the end you'll begin to wonder what there ever was to be afraid of.'

3

RETRIBUTION

For the time being, Larry elected to stay at the Bar-6. His offer to pay for his keep declined, he turned instead to doing whatever odd jobs were necessary, spending the rest of his time with Val whilst she gave him lessons in marksmanship and horse-riding. There seemed to be nothing of which she was afraid. She had all the vigour and freshness of the great spaces in which she had been reared – yet she still managed to stay feminine.

Each day she selected one particular spot about a mile from the ranch, where, in peace, she and Larry could indulge in gunfire without the fear of panicking any of the Bar-6 steers. And, by degrees, Larry's aim began to improve. At the end of a week – which had been remarkably peaceful as far as incursions by Cliff Makin were concerned – he was a passably good shot with a .45.

'I've a long way to go before I'm anywhere near as good as you, Val,' he confessed, as they took a rest at the side of the trail.

'Don't be too sure,' the girl replied, her eyes fixed on the cobalt sky. 'You're coming along nicely. The point is, Larry, does the handling of a gun make you feel any more confident?'

'Not really.' Larry sighed. 'But I've made up my mind that I'm not going back home. I'm staying out here to try and reclaim my inheritance.'

'I'm glad of that,' the girl said, gripping his arm. Their eyes met for a moment, then Larry looked away, almost shyly.

'Hence my learning how to handle a gun,' he said. 'I have two matters to take up with Makin. One is an apology to you, and the other is my inheritance. If I can get him at the point of a gun, maybe I'll be able to manage something. Just a few more days; then I'll try my luck. Incidentally, I'm surprised he hasn't been round to pester you again.'

'Perhaps he's finally got the message I gave him in the saloon. Anyway, whatever the explanation, the longer he stays away the better. Now, come on: you've a lot more practice to do.'

So Larry continued to learn under the girl's expert tuition, and three days later, after breakfast, he rode into town with a .45 at his hip, fully prepared to try and knock some of the conceit out of Makin, and also make him admit that he had pulled a legal double-cross in regard to the Double-L spread.

Larry, however, was something of a pot lion. As long as he had stayed away from the town and had Val's encouragement, he had felt he could move mountains. Now, tying his horse to the rail outside Makin's office, he was plagued by doubts.

He looked about him at the busy boardwalks, the wagons and horsemen moving up and down the street. Then, his hand on the .45, he strode up the steps to Makin's office. Here and there a curious glance was cast at him. In his grey suit and soft hat he was still remembered as the 'dude', the tenderfoot who had beaten the best card-player in town at poker.

With his hand on the knob of the outer door, Larry hesitated, suddenly assailed by doubts as to his ability to subdue the powerful Makin.

'Well, if it ain't the paleface dude!'

Larry started and turned. Two punchers had come up behind him on the boardwalk. Dimly he remembered having seen their faces in the Lucky Dollar – two of Makin's henchmen!

'Want a word with the boss?' asked the one who had spoken.

'Sure he does,' the other said, grinning widely. 'What's stopping you stridin' into the office, pantie-waist? Feelin' kinda leery at meetin' the boss?'

'I've finished my business with him,' Larry said quickly, and turned to go but the nearer cowpuncher caught his arm and swung him back.

'No, you don't, yeller belly! You can't have seen the boss – he told us he'd fix you good if he ever saw you in town again – and right now you're still standin'! *Git in there an' see him!*'

Seized by the collar of his jacket, Larry was dragged into the office as the door was flung open for him. He came up with a gasp against the tall filing-cabinet, the two punchers lounging in after him. At the roll-top, Cliff Makin looked up in astonishment, then grinned round his cheroot.

'We found him outside tryin' to make up his mind whether to come in or not so we did it for him, boss,' one of the punchers said contemptuously.

'You did right.' Makin was almost purring. Then he added more sharply: 'What brought you boys here?'

'Just bringing these reports from the Double-L,' said the second man, handing them over.

'From my ranch, you mean,' Larry said, straightening up.

'Shut your mouth!' Makin glared at him and then tossed the papers on his desk. 'I'm glad you two jiggers are here – it'll save me the job of fixing this guy! Since he evidently didn't get out of the district when I told him to, the only way is to make him too ashamed to stop.'

Larry's hand twitched to get at his .45, only he didn't have the nerve with the eyes of the three men fixed on him. Then Makin came out from behind his desk.

'Since you haven't left, you've no doubt muscled in nicely with Val King. Taken her from me, in fact. Having lost my hold on her when I lost the deeds to the Bar-6, there didn't seem much point in looking her up too soon. Now I'm intending to take action – starting with eradicating you before you cramp my style too much.'

'Better go easy on killin' him, boss,' one of the punchers warned. 'Be difficult to cover up now everyone in town knows him—'

'I'm not wastin' no good slugs on this critter: I'm just going to make him too big a laughing-stock to stay around. Hank, you'll find a pot of yellow paint in the cupboard there, and a brush. Get them.'

Hank did as he was told. He set them on the desk and waited for the next move. Makin grinned widely; then he suddenly snatched Larry's .45 from him and threw it aside. Next he delivered a smashing uppercut that banged Larry's head violently against the metal cabinet. His senses swimming, Larry was helpless to prevent Makin from tearing his coat off and the shirt from his back, leaving him only in trousers and singlet.

Held tightly by the two punchers, he had to submit as Makin very deliberately painted a huge Y in yellow paint across the front of his singlet; then he did the same with the back before tossing the brush back in the pot.

'Around here all the folks know that means yellow,' Makin said coldly. 'If you can stay here and live this down you're better than I thought. OK, Hank – throw him out!'

Larry was grabbed again and then flung savagely through the open doorway. He crashed down the three steps from the boardwalk to the street and lay in the dust for a moment. It was the sound of raucous laughter that made him finally scramble to his feet.

Punchers lining the boardwalk had noticed the clean yellow Y on his back and the dirt-caked one on his chest. Larry reeled in the direction of his horse, and then paused as a bullet blew the dust from his feet an inch or so in front of him.

'Keep going, son,' Makin called to him, leaning over the rail. 'That's why you're all nicely painted up. Go on – *start dancing!*'

He fired again, and Larry jumped back quickly. After that he had to keep moving, and fast, as another bullet exploded inches from his heels. Then the loud rattle of a buckboard made him lunge desperately to one side – straight into the path of another one coming from the opposite direction.

40

Larry felt a tearing pain in his head and side, then he was flung over and over in the dust, the wagon wheels bouncing sickeningly over his writhing body. Then came merciful oblivion.

The first person to react was Makin, dodging back quickly into his office when he saw the accident. He had no wish to be indicted as the man who had caused Larry to be knocked over. Not that the sheriff would ever dare to bring such a charge, but the townsfolk might.

Most of them were too concerned over Larry's inert body to bother about the cause of the trouble, however. He was lifted gently and carried into the general stores; then the rider of the buckboard came in, carrying a small bag. The fact that he was Doc Barnes, the one medico Buzzard's Bend possessed, was at least fortunate for Larry.

For Larry himself things did not begin to make sense until he realized that he was in a room with half-drawn shades, lying in a cool, comfortable bed and looking at the profile of Val as she bent her head over some needlework. He stirred very slowly, then winced.

'Hello, Val,' he whispered.

Immediately she put down her needlework and her eyes brightened in sudden joy. Getting up she rushed to the door and opened it.

'Dad!' she called. 'Dad – he's recovered consciousness. Come on – quickly!'

Returning to Larry's side she caught at his hand as it lay on the coverlet. 'How are you feeling?' she asked gently.

'Like I've been kicked by a mule,' Larry muttered, and realized that his head and ribs were bandaged. 'I remember being run over a wagon . . . what happened after that?'

'Plenty, Larry. But don't talk now. You've been very ill.'

'I *want* to talk,' he insisted. 'I've no idea what's been going on, and. . . .'

He stopped as Richard King came into the bedroom, carrying a bowl of steaming soup on a tray. He sat down at the bedside, lowered a spoon in the soup, and held it forth for Larry to drink.

'All kept ready for when you recovered,' he explained. 'Come on, son – drink it.'

It was hot and tasted of beef. By the time Larry had consumed the contents of the bowl he was feeling a good deal stronger, though every movement made him wince.

'You've been in a bad way,' King said, somewhat tactlessly. 'You got a wallop on the skull, two broken ribs, bruising and lacerations. Blow on the head was worst.'

Larry was silent, frowning in perplexity at his apparent memory loss.

'It sure was providential that the wagon that ran you down was being driven by Doc Barnes. You might easily have died without his immediate ministrations. But he reckons that, in time, you'll be back to your old self.'

A strange expression seemed to cross Larry's face at these words. Val interpreted it as tiredness.

'That's enough for now, Dad.' She looked at Larry as he lay in the bed. 'You need to rest. . . .'

But Larry was already asleep.

Two hours later he awoke; then he went to sleep again after more nourishment. The pattern was repeated over the following days, but gradually broken tissues began to heal themselves; slowly his sleeping-periods became less and less. A month after his accident, he was on the ranch house veranda in a chair, a rug round his knees, the blaze of the Arizona summer sun filling him with new life. Beside him, as always, sat Val King.

'I can't tell you, Val, how grateful I am for all you've done for me,' he said quietly, reaching out his hand and grasping her shoulder. 'Especially as I was a stranger.'

'Hardly a stranger, Larry.' Val smiled. 'You ceased to be that from the moment you recovered the ranch for us. The main thing now is that you've pulled through. You're getting stronger every day, putting on weight. You'll soon be around with the best of us.'

'I guess so,' he agreed, looking into the sunny expanse, his hand still about the girl's shoulder.

Val studied him covertly. She was trying to resolve what there was that was different about him. He looked drawn from his ordeal. But there was something there that had not been apparent before. A firmness about his mouth and chin, a curious light in his eyes as though . . . Val dropped her gaze as he turned suddenly.

'Makin been round in the interval?' he asked.

'Briefly – once or twice. I think he only came to find out if you were alive or not. He caused your accident, didn't he? We heard that from some of the townsfolk.'

'He caused it, yes,' Larry assented, a curious tightness about his lips. 'How did he treat you?'

'Roughly – as usual. He only left me alone when Dad threatened to pump lead into him. Seems as though he doesn't mean to be shaken off.'

Larry did not say any more. He relaxed and gave himself up to thought. He came out of a deep reverie to find Val had brought him coffee and sandwiches.

'You're an angel,' he said, smiling. 'Sit down a minute, Val. I want to tell you something. . . .'

43

She promptly did so, holding the sandwich plate for him.

'I've had plenty of time to think things through, since the accident. Because of Makin, I very nearly died. And if I *had* died, then Makin would have found a way to blight your life, and that of your father. In fact, he may yet try to do just that.'

'But you *didn't* die,' Val pointed out, puzzled as to where the conversation was leading.

'It would have been my own fault if I had,' Larry said frankly. 'I came here as an Englishman, completely ignorant of the ways of the West. A fish out of water. I failed to adapt, and because of that I nearly died.' Throwing the rug from his knees, he got to his feet and walked slowly to the porch rail. Gripping it, he stood, looking out over the pasturelands, drenched in the fierce heat of the summer sun. Val drifted to his side, quite unable to analyse his mood.

'Something the matter, Larry?' she asked.

'Yes . . .' He turned and gave her such a direct look she was startled for a moment. 'You're looking at a new Larry Ashfield, Val. Not the man who got thrown into a horsetrough and accepted insults; not the one who was afraid to draw his gun; not the one who had yellow paint on his chest and back. I've found something I never knew I had, and I owe it to you and your dad to put it to use.'

Val shrugged, still puzzled at his meaning.

'We only did what anybody would do.'

'Do you suppose,' Larry asked slowly, 'that if I can get my ranch and gold mine back from Makin, you might consider marrying me?'

Val only smiled. She did not need to give an answer.

'I can't ask you until then,' Larry said. 'I've nothing to offer. But the Double-L and the gold mine are worth a fortune combined. Until I've got them I wouldn't dream of asking you to take on a load of trouble.'

'Isn't a wife supposed to share her husband's troubles?'

'Normal ones, perhaps – not bullets and fists and death.' Larry gazed fixedly into the sunlight. 'That's what my affairs may come to before I've settled them. I have so much to deal with, so many accounts to square.'

The passing of the blazing days finally convinced Val – and in a less personal way her father – that Larry Ashfield was definitely a new man. The hours he spent in the sunlight, gradually doing heavier jobs as his strength increased, turned his grey, drab skin to a deep brick-red, and then to nut brown. His shoulders, which had always been fairly broad even if fleshless, began to thicken. He began to gain weight rapidly.

There came a day when Larry realized he was two stones heavier than he had been on his arrival in Buzzard's Bend, and he was feeling fitter than he had ever done in his life. He was attuned to the blazing climate, self-confident, nursing only one burning desire – to avenge the insults and abuse that had been heaped upon him.

Just over two months after his accident he rode into town one evening, and dismounted at the Lucky Dollar. None of the lounging cowpunchers recognized him in his riding-pants, half-boots, check shirt, orange kerchief, and Stetson hat. He looked like a tall, broad-shouldered man of the trail who had blown into town for a drink.

He pushed open the batwings of the saloon and looked about him upon the usual men and women at the tables, the haze of tobacco smoke, the distant gambling habitués. He received one or two glances; nothing more. So, his hand resting lightly on the butt of the new .45 he had bought – from the $5,000 he had won from Makin – he strolled across to the bar-counter and ordered whiskey.

The bartender gave it to him and looked as though he were trying to remember something. For that matter Cliff Makin, seated with his chief henchman, Hank, at a distant table, was also trying to remember something. When the truth dawned on him he nearly dropped his whiskey glass.

'Sweet hell,' he breathed, staring. 'Hank, that guy at the bar over there! It's our little playmate come back! Larry Ashfield.'

Hank stared fixedly, took a quick drink, and stared again.

'What in heck's happened to the critter? He looks as big as a house.'

'Been lazing around and stuffing himself after that fall he took,' Makin decided sourly. 'He's filled out a little, but I guess a leopard can't change its spots. I wonder what his game is?'

Hank grinned. 'Mebbe he'd like another walk around town with a yellow Y on his belly?'

'Get over there pronto and sound him out. Let him know he ain't welcome.'

'Sure thing, boss.' Hank got to his feet, hitched up his gun belt, then strolled over to where Larry was leaning one elbow on the bar.

'Howdy,' Hank said briefly, grinning. 'Remember me?'

'Yes, I remember you,' Larry said, fixing the man with a discomfiting stare. 'You were the one who threw me out of

46

Makin's office the day he painted a Y on my singlet. After that I got run over.'

'We didn't figure on that happenin',' Hank explained. 'Have a drink?'

'I've got one. What is it you really want?' Larry's tone was hard and uncompromising, and instinctively his hand strayed to the comforting butt of his gun.

'The boss told me to tell you that you're not wanted. If you don't quit town and stop crampin' his style, you'll be thrown out.'

Larry said nothing. Slowly he finished his drink, then he held out his empty hand towards Hank. As he watched, Larry clenched his fist, and then opened it again. In his palm lay a large-sized duck's egg.

'Mighty neat,' Hank said, sensing this was not a good time to start making trouble.

'Very,' Larry agreed calmly. 'Take it home with you. Might make a pancake.'

Hank took it in his hand, then Larry suddenly reached out and crushed Hank's fingers. The egg squashed instantly, the yolk running gummily round his hand and on to his trousers. Somebody laughed, and it was not long before half a dozen others joined him. Scowling, Hank stared at his messy hand.

'And another,' Larry said, taking another huge duck egg from the back of Hank's dirty old hat.

Hank looked at it in fascination, then he suddenly found his hat whipped from his head and the egg crashed on the top of his skull. He swore thickly and clutched at his gun.

'Yellow,' Larry explained. 'Like the paint I had daubed on me. Now get back to that swaggering boss of yours and tell him that if he's anything to say to me he can say it himself. You might add I'll have plenty to say to him before I leave this saloon. That's why I'm here.'

'You cheap, lily-white tenderfoot!' Hank howled, pulling out his gun, yolk running down his hair and face. 'You can't do—'

His words were jolted clean back into his throat as a smashing right-hander took him under the jaw. His gun went flying. Half-lifted from his feet, he collided with the table behind him, overturning it. Dazedly, he collapsed in a smother of broken glass and flowing liquor.

'On your way,' Larry said coldly, his own gun at the ready.

Sticky, furious, his jaw throbbing, Hank got slowly on his feet. He recovered his gun and pushed it in its holster; then, with a startled glance over his shoulder, he returned to the table where Makin had been watching the proceedings in blank astonishment, along with most of the saloon customers.

'Boss, the guy's loco,' Hank panted. 'He brought some rotten eggs from some place and smashed 'em on me! Look at me—'

'I don't need to; you stink a mile off.' Makin got to his feet, kicking his chair out of the way. He strode across the saloon to where Larry was pouring out another drink.

As he neared the bar, he noted the filled-out shoulders, the brown skin, the obvious ripple of muscle beneath the shirtsleeves.

'This has gone far enough, Ashfield,' Makin growled.

'I don't think it has.' Larry smiled icily. 'I intend to stick around town until I've made you hand over the property you've stolen from me.'

Makin narrowed his eyes. 'I don't think that even you

are idiot enough to try conclusions with me, feller!'

'I intend doing just that, Makin. But first, there's the matter of your upsetting Val King's peace of mind. . . .'

Makin saw the danger light in Larry's grey eyes, even if he could not understand it. His hand blurred down to his own gun – then he stopped in mid-action, spluttering and cursing as the contents of Larry's whiskey glass landed right in his face.

He was temporarily blinded as the spirit burned his eyes – then a hammer blow on the nose sent him sprawling along the bar counter. Dazedly, he was aware of a trickle of blood warm his upper lip. It spurred him to sudden, desperate retaliatory action. He forgot all about his gun and lashed out his fist. It missed Larry's ear by a fraction, and a split second later Larry's left fist came up with all the power of his arm. It smacked into Makin's jaw. With a gasp he clutched at the counter, missed, and landed on his face in the sawdust. Before he could get up a knee was in the centre of his spine and a forearm under his aching chin.

'All right, Makin,' Larry said, his voice unhurried. 'We'll have the apology for Miss King first, shall we? I know she isn't present, but the rest of these good people are witness to your statements.'

'You blasted skunk!' Makin panted, striving to free himself. 'I'm not apologizing to anybody! Val was my girl before you showed up, and still is—'

'No she isn't,' Larry said, and began to increase his arm lock. He only stopped when Makin, his face streaming with tears and perspiration, screamed from the pain in his back.

'Say it!' Larry snapped. 'You've molested her for the last

time. Say you're sorry for it, and that you'll never go near her again.'

Makin breathed hard, his hands clawing in the sawdust, spots of blood falling from his battered nose. Then he found his chin rising again and his back bending.

'*All right*!' he shrieked abruptly. 'I apologize! I moved outa turn . . . I'll not go near Val any more.'

'Good,' Larry said. 'Break your promise and I'll break your neck. Now get up.'

Slowly and painfully, Makin got to his feet. Grinning faces on all sides did not improve his temper. And he was baffled – completely so. Larry Ashfield had either got a twin brother of unexpected toughness, or else must have been soft-pedalling himself in the first instance. . . .

'There's something else,' Larry said, hooking his thumbs on his gun-belt. 'I mean my ranch and that gold mine.'

'That's all legally fixed up,' Makin retorted, snatching up his fallen hat. 'I told you about the debts your uncle contracted.'

Larry's hand shot out suddenly and gripped the front of Makin's shirt.

'I know I've been cheated, Makin – or gypped, as you call it around here – and I'm going to straighten it out if I have to tear you in pieces to do it. Now, tell me what really happened when you handed things over to this Simon Galt, who's taken my place.'

Makin's only response was a cynical grin. He turned his back in contempt – then he suddenly found himself advancing at tremendous speed, a hand at his collar and pants. He was bundled through the batwings and out into the street, followed by the interested customers from the saloon. Cursing and struggling, he was forced onwards, until he reached the horse trough. Realizing what was coming, he dug in his heels, and forced himself to turn.

He knew it was a wrong move when he absorbed a haymaker to the mouth, jarring his teeth. More blows followed it. Lost to all sense of balance, and feeling as if his head was exploding, Makin dropped full length in the water trough. The shock of the water revived him somewhat, but as he tried to scramble free, Larry's hand locked in his thick hair and forced his head under the water again.

'Admit those deeds were faked,' Larry demanded, as he brought his head up momentarily for air.

Makin spluttered and choked and said nothing so Larry jammed his head under the water again.

'You gypped me, didn't you?' Larry snapped, bringing his head up again.

Makin might well have made some kind of answer – but he was not given the opportunity, as there came a sudden interruption. Sheriff Crawford pushed his way through the crowd, his revolver in his hand.

'*That's enough, Ashfield!*'

Larry looked up in surprise. The sheriff was a tubby, narrow-eyed man with a thin, unpleasant nose. That he was one of Cliff Makin's closest friends – along with the town mayor – was common knowledge.

'Who says it is?' Larry demanded bluntly.

'Leave him be, Sheriff,' somebody complained. 'It's about time Makin had the tar beaten outa him.'

'I've got law and order to preserve!' Crawford snapped, looking about him. 'When it comes to near drowning a man to make him confess to something he never did, it's time to call a halt.'

51

Makin sat on the edge of the trough, his clothes cling-ing to him, his face puffed from the blows he had received.

'About time you showed up!' he commented sourly. 'Sooner you get this louse locked up for assault, the better.'

Crawford hesitated, acutely aware that the temper of the people would never permit him to try and put Larry in jail. Instead:

'We'll call it a fight and let it go at that,' Crawford decided. 'You'd better be on your way, Ashfield, and don't try getting tough around here again.'

Larry hesitated, then he shrugged.

'Nice of you to step in and save your pardner,' he said briefly. 'It won't stop me dealing with him somewhere else – just when he least expects it.'

With that Larry pushed through the crowd, and returned to his horse up the street. Disappointed at the tame finish to everything, the spectators broke up and began drifting back towards the Lucky Dollar. Makin watched them go, then stood up.

'Thanks,' he said briefly to the sheriff. 'Something's happened to that guy since he was last around: he's dyna-mite! He'll have to be taken care of – and pronto. Get Hank and the boys to fix it.' He broke off in disgust. 'I've got to be rid of these wet things.'

The sheriff nodded grimly and turned away. As he moved back in the direction of the saloon Larry came riding past, heading out of town for the trail. Not three minutes after him six men also went riding, and at the tremendous speed at which they travelled in the starlight they got ahead of Larry before he could reach the Bar-6.

His first intimation of them was when they suddenly emerged from the side of the trail, blocking his path. He reined to a halt, his hand dropping to his gun. Then a warning voice stopped his action.

'You're covered, Ashfield. Stay right where you are!'

Larry obeyed. He recognized Hank as he came forward in the starlight. He reached out a hand, and Larry found his gun taken from him.

'Far as I'm concerned, feller, you'd be a lot safer dead than alive. But it ain't going to be by bullets. The boss is careful about things like that. Bullets can be traced back to their owners sometimes, and it won't do. . . . But there's another way to take care of you. You're comin' with us to Eagle's Pass.'

Larry knew of the spot vaguely – about five miles south of the Bar-6 at the foot of the mountain range.

'Start ridin',' Hank ordered. 'And don't try any tricks, or you'll suffer for them.'

Larry could do nothing but comply. On and on through the pastureland, through the ground-level mists . . . until, by the time the moon had risen, they had left the green countryside behind and were riding amidst dusty earth and rock chippings on the outskirts of the mountain foothills.

The mountains reared grey and invulnerable into the starry sky, their peaks lost in the glittering diadem of light above them. Rock walls closed in as the horsemen left the immediate foothills behind and began to follow a narrow arroyo that led eventually into a canyon.

'This is it,' Hank said, calling a halt. 'Just the spot we need. Hey, Ashfield! See them cedar trees up the canyon side there?'

The trees were visible as a darker mass against the

53

canyon face. Larry saw them but said nothing.

'There's plenty of dry brushwood below 'em,' Hank continued, 'and a nice draught blowing through this canyon. With you bound to one of them higher trees, and the brushwood fired, there won't be much to save you gettin' nicely fried, I reckon! Nobody likely to find you in this remote spot, neither!'

Larry was forced to descend from his horse. He remained silent and passive whilst his wrists were secured behind him with lariat rope.

'Start climbin',' Hank ordered, brandishing his gun.

Larry found the ascent difficult with his hands bound, but where he could not climb he was dragged, and so gradually he was brought to a spot perhaps a hundred feet above the canyon floor, in the midst of a sloping hillside wood of dense cedar trees. Up here they swayed in the cold night wind, their leaves rustling.

He said nothing as his wrists were fastened securely at the back of the tree; then his ankles were also bound. By the time Hank had finished his handiwork he was satisfied that Larry could not budge.

'OK, boys, let's go.' Hank grinned wolfishly. 'We've a fire to start.'

He and his men turned away, hurrying through the shadowy gloom of the trees, until at length they and the sound of their movements were lost. Only then did Larry withdraw his wrists from the ropes tethering them round the tree. He smiled to himself.

'Maybe learning magic is going to prove more useful than I thought,' he muttered, and stooped to unfasten his ankles.

Magic had not released his wrists. He had merely used

54

the old magician's trick of keeping his wrists slightly apart by wedging his thumb between them as they had been bound. The dim light had made it quite impossible for Hank to detect the subterfuge.

By the time Larry had his ankles freed he saw the first glowing flame below, announcing that the brushwood had been set on fire. Fanned by the wind, the flames spread immediately, feeding avidly on the sun-parched leaves and branches of the trees above. Within thirty seconds a column of flame was devouring its way up the cliffside, hurling a fountain of crackling sparks into the night.

For Larry to go below was impossible: he would be ringed by fire. Climbing upwards beyond the timberline would be tough, and he would have to move fast to keep ahead of the flames. But it was the only way out, so he began to climb swiftly, digging his toes and fingers into the rockery, using the tree boles to thrust himself upwards.

Even so the fire was gaining, a crackling inferno streaming up in his wake, the trees exploding like monstrous torches as they burst into vivid flame.

Larry began to fear for his chances of escaping, until the glare of the flames revealed the unexpected. Not very far above him there was a black, irregular hole in the cliff in fact, not one, but several. Evidently they were ancient blow-holes, cave mouths, created in the mountains by volcanic action in the dim past. There lay sanctuary.

Larry made a desperate effort, scrambling upwards, pursued by a curtain of fire. He reached the ledge of the cave nearest to him and clawed his way over it. Within seconds he was inside the cave, backing into its depths, watching the increasing glare outside as the flames came roaring nearer,

4

DEATH AT THE BAR-6

The fire reached the cave, the flames and smoke belching around the opening as the trees near it fused, exploded and crackled. Larry, deep inside the rocky sanctuary, was untouched. Gradually, the inferno began to pass by as it burned its way to the very limits of the timberline. Before it was spent it might involve entire swathes of vegetation in the region – there was no escape for Larry just yet, unless he wished to wade ankle-deep in red-hot ashes.

So he turned and surveyed the cave into which he had come. The light of the rising moon, penetrating the smoke wreaths, was just strong enough to show him that he was in a tunnel, not a cave. A black abyss yawned at the back of the place, and from somewhere in its depths came a remote bumping sound, some kind of buried concussion as though a pile-driver were at work.

Larry hesitated. His interest was aroused, but so was his

sense of caution. He had no gun with which to defend himself if he ran into trouble. He began to walk forward very slowly into the depths, presently taking a box of lucifers from his pocket as the blackness became absolute.

The heavy dust was undisturbed and lay deep, so evidently nobody had passed this way recently. He was glad of it in one sense: it muffled his advance if there did happen to be anybody unpleasant at the end of the journey.

And the further he went into the heart of the mountain range the more the distant concussions impressed him. He could tell that they were created mechanically by the regular intervals of silence between the reverberations.

Then, as he found that everything was not entirely dark ahead, he advanced more stealthily as the distant glow of grey turned to a golden-yellow. He reached a ledge of rock and peered over it into an enormous natural cavern lighted by batteries of oil-lamps, all of them training their glare on a gang of sweating men, toiling at the rock face. Not far from them a mechanical driller was pounding at the granite and creating the concussions that Larry had heard.

Intrigued, he lay watching, hidden in the deep shadows. The walls of the cavern were lined with rich yellow veins, suggesting gold-bearing ores. He realized he was in his own mine, the one Cliff Makin had taken away from him. Now that he came to see the enormous value of the mine – which seemed to Larry as though it might have been some leftover cavern from the days of the gold-hoarding Aztecs – he could almost understand Makin's duplicity. Any man in his position would have found it difficult to let such a prize escape from him.

Larry continued watching the activity for some time. There were portable wooden dwellings, all manner of equipment, and gangs of men hard at work. With the whole operation obviously so well organized, Larry knew that, unarmed as he was, there was nothing he could attempt at the moment. All he could do now was to return the way he had come, and try and find his way back to the Bar-6. But at a later date. . . .

And meanwhile, back at Buzzard's Bend, Makin himself was riding out of the town. His various injuries patched up and wearing a fresh outfit, he had just received the information from Hank as to how Larry Ashfield had been eliminated. Now in distinctly better spirits, he was resolved to bring things to a head with Val King.

Reaching the Bar-6, he pounded heavily on the locked outer screen door. It was Val herself who promptly answered, having fallen into the error of thinking it was Larry who had returned. She stepped back quickly into the gloom of the hall as she recognized the voice of Makin.

'Howdy, Val! Surprised, huh?'

'What do *you* want?' she demanded angrily. 'I've told you enough times to stop pestering me—'

'Get in the living-room,' Makin snapped, kicking the door shut behind him. 'I've a few things to tell you. . . .'

Grabbing her arm, he forced her before him into the oil-lit glow of the room. Richard King had recognized Makin's voice, and stood ready with his gun levelled.

'Get the hell outa here, Makin,' he said deliberately, 'unless you want to be shot as a trespasser. Come over here, Val, where you're safe.'

As the girl tried to obey Makin tightened his grip on

58

her arm and swung her in front of him.

'OK, King,' he said briefly. 'If you want to shoot me you can shoot through Val. Otherwise, put that gun down!' King lowered his weapon slightly, but did not lay it aside.

Makin's own gun suddenly leapt into his free hand. He fired deliberately, and King gave a gasp. His gun dropped and he stared fixedly for a moment at blood brimming from his torn palm. Apparently the slug had gone clean through it.

'Dad!' Val cried in horror, trying to break away. 'You're hurt! Cliff, you murdering swine—'

'Shut up!' he interrupted her. 'Your old man shouldn't play games if he doesn't want to get hurt. Better get your hand bound up, King – you're losing blood fast.'

His face set hard in the lamplight, King sat down slowly and then pulled his kerchief from his neck with his uninjured hand. Using his teeth to help him, he wrapped up his damaged palm.

'One day, Makin, I'll return this – with interest. And let Val go, damn you!'

'When I'm ready.' Makin was still being cautious. 'I just thought you'd like to know, Val, that I had to take care of your boyfriend. I don't know what you've done to him in the interval, but he sure acted as though he owned Buzzard's Bend. It became necessary to tone him down.'

'By doing what?' Val tore free of Makin's grip and glared at him.

'Hank and the boys fixed him,' Makin said, his eyes cold. 'He met with an "accident", same as most clever guys do around here.'

'You've *killed* him!' Val whispered, her eyes wide in horror.

'Put that way it sounds unpleasant.' Makin grinned. 'But I guess it adds up to the same thing.'

Words were beyond Val. She stood looking at Makin as though he were some kind of venomous snake. Her father's gaze moved slightly, however, to the gloom of the hall beyond the open living-room door. He saw a figure glide across it and then vanish. It was his Indian servant, who had evidently heard the voices and the shot. Possibly he had gone to fetch the ranch foreman and his boys from the bunkhouse.

'Do you realize,' King asked deliberately, holding his damaged hand, 'that you're admitting to murder in the presence of witnesses?'

'You can talk all you like, King, but it won't do you any good without a second witness. And the second witness being Val, that lets me out. A wife can't testify against her husband!'

'*What* did you say?' Val looked up sharply from an agitated contemplation of her father. 'Have you gone crazy?'

'Mebbe it won't be for love,' Makin admitted, with a cynical grin. 'Just the same, you'll marry me, Val – because the alternative is that you'll lose your father!'

'I reckon you've gone trigger-happy, Makin,' King said. 'Having fixed Larry, you think you can fix me just the same.'

'I *know* I can.' Makin twirled his gun in his fingers. 'You're too winged at the moment to fight back, and I've plenty of bullets left in this gun. Before I left town, Val, I fixed it with Luke Clay to come over here in another half-hour. He'll perform the marriage service. He'll bring his wife and daughter as witnesses.'

Val moved to a chair and sat down shakily. Luke Clay was the local blacksmith and preacher. When he was not shoeing horses he was ministering to the soul.

'You think a decent-living man like Clay will ever marry us when I tell him the facts?' she asked. 'After I tell him everything you've done?'

'Are you deliberately trying to kill your father?' Makin demanded, still toying with his gun. 'Another word out of place, Val, and your father gets it.'

'Even you haven't the damned nerve to shoot me dead with a minister and two other witnesses in the room,' King snapped. 'You'd swing in double-quick time!'

'I'd probably swing anyway if Val talked too much,' Makin answered, 'so I'd take that risk.' He relaxed a little and grinned. 'Nobody need get hurt. I've simply removed the opposition, and now I just want you to be my wife, Val. Simple, isn't it?'

She gave him a look of disgust, and suddenly her father, sensing Makin was distracted, stooped towards his fallen gun. Instantly Makin's hard voice checked him.

'Hold it, King! Better leave that where it is!'

He strode over to the gun, picked it up, then tossed it into a far corner of the shadowy room. Returning to the table, he perched himself on the edge of it, his gun cocked.

'All we have to do now is to wait for the preacher.'

Silence fell. With his free hand Makin took a cheroot from his pocket. He struck a lucifer along the edge of the table and inhaled deeply at the weed. King looked about him anxiously, wondering just where his servant had gone.

'Surprising how the time drags when you're waiting for something exciting to happen,' Makin commented, after

61

a long interval. 'Gives me the chance to tell you just what I've figured out for you and me, Val.'

'I'm not interested,' she said bitterly.

'I am,' a voice said from the doorway – and Makin swung round, levelling his gun simultaneously. Before he could fire a heavy object shot through the air and struck him violently on the side of the head, making him slip from the edge of the table. He found his wrist being seized and twisted violently. The savage pain caused the weapon to clatter to the table top.

'Surprised?' Larry enquired drily, his eyes glinting in the lamplight as he tossed Makin's gun further aside.

'Larry!' Val cried joyously, leaping up. 'He said you were dead!'

'Trifle premature, Makin, eh?' Larry asked, his fists clenching as the lawyer stood glaring at him. 'You thought I went up in a blaze of glory at Eagle's Pass, but I escaped, and luck was with me – I found my horse running round in circles trying to find me. After that, it didn't take me long to get back here.'

'Hank said he'd lost track of your horse,' Makin said, recovering himself. 'In fact I think Hank rather lost his head. I only told him to run you out of town.'

'Don't try lying, Makin,' Larry snapped. 'And you were told to keep away from this spread.'

'So I didn't.' Makin shrugged. 'And I never shall whilst Val is around. I've a preacher on his way here to marry us.'

'Pity he'll have a wasted journey,' Richard King said, getting to his feet. Larry's eyes travelled to the blood-stained kerchief about the rancher's hand; then he looked at Val.

'Better take your dad in the kitchen and bind him up

properly,' he said. 'His hand wants fixing – and besides you may not like to see what's going to happen in here.'

'With what?' Makin asked sourly, glancing at the floor. 'I reckon you've no more stones to throw at me.'

'I don't need them,' Larry said evenly, throwing his hat into a corner. 'Go on, Val – take your father out.'

She hesitated, then her father decided the issue for her by leaving the room. She gave an anxious backwards glance. Larry did not notice it. He was measuring Makin as he stood with clenched fists on the other side of the table.

'You're finished around here, Makin,' Larry said. 'I'm going to give you a sample of what you'll get any time you set foot in here again, until maybe my patience gets exhausted and I put a bullet through you instead. . . .'

Makin remained silent. He kept his eyes fixed on Larry's clenched fists.

'I'm going to give you some long-overdue repayment for molesting Val and shooting her father, not to mention what you tried to do to me,' Larry explained. 'By doing so, I can soften you up so that when the minister comes he can be a witness to the statement you're going to make concerning my stolen property. Once I have a minister as a witness, it won't take me very long to get my case tried by Judge Gascoigne, who's one of the few straight officials in Buzzard's Bend. In other words, Makin, I aim to finish what I began earlier tonight when your beloved sheriff stepped in and helped you. . . .'

Suddenly Makin made his move, and lashed up his big right fist with all the strength of his arm. It struck Larry under the jaw, and he lurched back, sitting down unexpectedly in the chair behind him. In one lunge, Makin was across the desk, raining blows down on Larry's face and head before he had a chance to rise.

Larry did the only thing he could. He buckled up his knees and thrust outwards with all his power. The blow struck Makin in the midriff, doubling him up – then he straightened again as a left whizzed up under his chin and made him bite the end of his tongue. A fist crashing against his ear sent him spinning round.

Head singing, he hit the wall, but used it to rebound himself and came charging forward. Larry held back, waiting to deliver a killing uppercut, but he mistimed by a fraction. Makin's bunched fist slammed into his nose, and hurtled him helplessly into the fireplace. He gasped and lunged clear as his hand was scorched momentarily by the flames – then Makin was upon him, squeezing at his throat with steel-strong fingers, trying to force his head back towards the flames.

Larry twisted and writhed, the heat searing the side of his face. Makin's own features were sweating, his hair wild, blood trickling from the nipped end of his tongue. Meeting Larry's desperate resistance at being pushed firewards, he paused for a split second and snatched up the heavy iron poker from the hearth, bringing it down with blinding force.

Larry twisted savagely. The poker crashed into the rough tile-work and fractured it. He heaved and arched his body, dislodging Makin's grip upon him. Flinging up his hands, he tore frenziedly at Makin's thick hair, dragging his head backwards. Then, holding the hair with one hand, he slammed down his fist repeatedly with the other. Both men fell to the floor, Larry on top.

Makin made his only move. He kicked up his right foot with all his power, slamming it in an arc so that the toe of his boot struck Larry on the back of his head. The blow caused Larry to lose his grip, and Makin instantly jabbed up his fist into Larry's face. He went reeling backwards, his teeth rattling, and sat down with a sickening bump.

But he was not too dazed to thrust up both his feet as Makin came hurtling upon him. The lawyer took the boots in his chest and cannoned backwards against the bureau. It stewed round under the impact, taking Makin with it as he clutched at it desperately.

As Larry flung himself towards him, his foot caught in a crumpled rug on the floor, and he pitched forward. Makin dived, hauled him to his feet, then swung him back against the wall and began to deliver the most savage punches he could muster. Dazed, feeling as if his brain were about to explode, Larry felt his senses trying to slide away. He did the only thing he could – dropped down suddenly so that Makin missed him and struck his fist agonizingly on the wall. Larry surged up again, gathering all his remaining strength for one terrific punch into Makin's already weakened stomach.

He gasped with the pain of the blow, and clapped his hands to his middle. Breathing was an agony; pressures beat like hammers before his eyes. Larry waited, gathering his remaining strength, and lashed up a haymaker that caught Makin clean under the chin and sent him staggering. Larry leaped after him, and his right hand thudded across Makin's face with savage violence. To Makin's dimming senses it seemed as though it had taken his nose with it. He hit the log wall, striking his head with such terrible force the universe blanked out in fiery stars. He sank to the floor and remained inert.

Breathless, his shirt in ribbons, hair fallen over his eyes,

Larry staggered to the table and clutched at it. For several seconds he could hardly move – then he realized that Val and her father had been watching from the doorway. Val came hurrying forward, her hands tenderly touching the streaks of blood across Larry's face and bare arms.

'I've still got the rest of the bandaging I used on Dad,' she said quickly, and turned to fetch it as her father came forward, smiling broadly.

'You've certainly learned how to fight, son! I reckon that'll show Makin that he isn't welcome around here.'

Larry could only grunt wearily, pushing his hair back from his forehead. King went over to Makin and prodded him with the toe of his boot.

'Time to wake up, Makin,' he said briefly.

Makin did not move. King frowned, dropping down on one knee as he shook the lawyer's shoulder. Getting no reaction, he did it more urgently; then he looked up from feeling Makin's chest carefully.

'Say, Larry, this guy's *dead*!' he exclaimed, startled.

Wincing from bruises, Larry went over to the fallen man and examined him quickly. There was no doubt he was dead – and the reason was not far to seek. Makin's head was at an acute angle. Obviously, in hitting the wall, he had broken his neck.

At that moment Val came back, with bandaging, a sponge, and a bowl of water on a tray. She set it on the table and then moved to where the two men kneeled.

'We can patch up Cliff afterwards, Larry. It's you I'm concerned about.'

'You can leave Cliff to the undertaker,' King said, with a grim glance. 'He's broken his neck, Val. Can't say I'm sorry, neither.'

Val just stood staring blankly; then at the sound of heavy feet in the hall she turned sharply. The two men looked up too as Sheriff Crawford and a couple of his deputies came into the room. Behind them was King's redskin servant.

'This what you meant?' Crawford asked, with a backward glance.

'Fight,' the Aztec said. 'Fight was getting bad. I thought I should fetch you. Makin had shot Mr King and was threatening to kill him.'

King got to his feet, dismissed the servant with a nod of his head, then looked at the paunchy Crawford. The sheriff's ferret-eyes studied the body on the floor.

'What's this?' he asked bluntly.

'Corpse,' Larry said, shrugging, and took the sponge from the tray to wipe blood from his face and arms.

For a moment Crawford and his two deputies fell to examining the body. Val and her father exchanged glances. Larry stood winding bandage round his scratched arm.

'I reckon this is murder,' Crawford said at length, turning.

'He was a trespasser,' King snapped. 'I had the right to shoot him – only he shot me first. Look at my hand. That Larry killed him instead of me, and that by accident, adds up to the same thing.'

'Not to me it doesn't,' Crawford said, taking out his gun. 'You admit you killed him, Ashfield?'

'Yes,' Larry admitted. 'Not deliberately, though. We were fighting, and he hit his head on the wall. The blow must have broken his neck.'

Crawford smiled thinly and glanced at his deputies.

'There you have it, boys. An admission of murder.'

'Self-defence,' Larry corrected. 'Don't start twisting things, Sheriff, because you were a friend of Makin's.'

'I'm not twisting anything. I've just had a definite statement from you that you murdered Makin, and my two deputies here will verify it. Their word and mine will be enough to convince any jury. Everybody in town knows that you and Makin didn't exactly love each other. That scrap you had in the high street will be used as evidence of it.'

'Just a minute, Sheriff,' King said deliberately. 'Are you trying to pin a murder rap on Larry?'

'I'm not trying, King, I'm *doing* it.' Crawford motioned with his gun. 'Finish getting yourself cleaned up, Ashfield, but stay where I can watch you. Then I'm taking you to the town jailhouse. I'm indicting you for murder, and I reckon you won't get away with a self-defence plea, either.'

'You've forgotten Val and her father,' Larry retorted. 'They can prove it.'

Crawford shrugged. 'Can you imagine a jury paying much attention to father and daughter, each obviously supporting the other? With two strangers you might have stood a chance: otherwise I don't think so. Now finish cleaning up.'

Val moved to tend the damage on Larry's face. She said nothing, but anxiety clearly showed in her expression. Then she paused as there came more sounds in the hall, where Luke Clay appeared, his wife and daughter behind him. They stopped on the threshold, taken aback by the unusual scene of a dead man on the floor, a blood-streaked one beside the table, and a sheriff and deputies with guns levelled.

'What do you want, Luke?' Crawford demanded.

The blacksmith scratched the back of his head.

'I reckon Mr Makin told me to get over here to perform a marriage ceremony. . . .'

'You can recite the last rites instead,' Crawford told him. 'And since you're the coroner around here, you can start making arrangements to get the body buried. I'm holding Larry Ashfield here as the killer.'

To Val and her father the ranch house seemed unbearably quiet when Larry had been taken away by the sheriff and Makin's body removed. Despite the late hour, Val had no thought of sleep. She paced restlessly up and down the living-room, watched by her father as he rested his injured hand on the table.

'No point in fretting yourself to a shadow like this, Val,' he said at last. 'Larry can only be tried by Judge Gascoigne, and he's one of the squarest men in town. That murder charge will never stick.'

'Won't it?' Val came to a halt beside the table, the lamp-light reflecting on to her troubled face. 'You know the kind of man Sheriff Crawford is. He's crooked, and always has been. Cliff was his closest friend, so naturally he'll do everything he can to get Larry a necktie party.'

'Agreed,' King admitted, smiling ruefully, 'but we'll have plenty to say, too. And Larry himself will put up a good fight.'

'Against a sheriff and two deputies who'll support him it may not be good enough,' Val said slowly. 'Everybody knows Larry and Cliff were enemies. That fact will tell against Larry.' She paused in her pacing, and spun round to look directly at her father.

'I think I know how we can make Larry safe. How do you suppose Crawford would get on if his two deputies – his only witnesses, remember – disappeared?'

As King pondered the question, Val came round the table and went on speaking urgently. 'I know both those deputies of Crawford's – Rog Lucas and Tom Harral. They're familiar about the town. I know where they live. They're single men who dig in together and work on one of the nearby spreads. Suppose we kidnapped them tonight?'

King smiled incredulously. 'How *can* we? Here am I with my gun hand ruined for some time to come, and—'

'I can handle guns,' she interrupted. 'I've yet to see any man try conclusions with six-shooters if he's on the wrong end of them. My idea is to get these deputies out of the way – and *keep* them out of the way – until after the trial. Without their biased testimony, which they only mean to give because Crawford has ordered them to – Larry ought to be able to get free.'

'Might just work at that,' King admitted, thinking. 'But what do you figure on doing with the men after you've got them?'

'Make them ride out to the mountain foothills. Nobody will ever find them there. You can stay and guard them easily enough, even if you are one-handed for the time being.'

'Sure thing, but you can't keep those men in the foothills for ever! The moment they are released they'll speed back into town and give their evidence.'

'Be too late then,' Val said. 'The judge can't reopen the trial once he's exonerated Larry. Be against the law.'

'Yeah – we hope,' King said uneasily. 'There is such a

70

thing as a retrial when fresh evidence comes in, but – OK,' he decided abruptly, 'we'll do it, Val. The only thing to decide is – when? We both need rest. We can't go through all that on top of what we've endured without some sleep. To attempt a stunt like this we need to be fresh.'

Val reflected. 'Well, maybe you're right,' she admitted, stifling a yawn. 'We can take it in spells, though.'

'Good enough. You go first. I'll wake you in a couple of hours.'

With a nod, Val kissed her father gently and then left the room. The fact that she now had some kind of plan in mind made her nerves calmer: she even managed to sleep for most of the two specified hours. Then her father took his turn until it was time for her to awaken him. It was still two hours from dawn when they were eating a quick break-fast of beans and coffee.

The eastern sky was still dark when they rode their horses along the trail to Buzzard's Bend, the town looking very much like a mausoleum at this unearthly hour. Val was wearing a leather mackinaw, shirt and riding pants, her hair flowing free.

'They live in that small wooden house at the far end of the street,' Val said, when the town was reached. 'I'd better go first since I can use both hands.'

She nudged her horse forward, alert for any signs of trouble, but all remained quiet. Gaining the wooden house at the end of the street they stopped their horses. Val dropped down from the saddle and took out her right-hand gun.

'Here I go,' she murmured, as her father also dismounted and moved closer. 'Keep me covered, Dad.'

King dodged down at the gatepost, his left-hand gun

71

ready for immediate action. Val mounted the short steps to the porch and looked about her in the gloom. Knowing the door would be locked, she moved silently to the side of the house and surveyed the lower windows. Two were tightly fastened; the one that was presumably that of the bedroom, was slightly open, top and bottom. She glided towards it, then paused as she spotted a bucket in the rear yard. She inverted it to use as a stand and found herself within easy reach of the window. For a while she crouched, listening to the sounds from within the room, until she was satisfied she could distinguish deep breathing. Only then did she raise her head and peer through the narrow gap of open window.

She was just able to make out the outlines of two beds, with two dark figures sleeping in them. She pushed the window up slowly, until she had room to throw one leg and then the other over the sill. She tiptoed across the room to the door, turned the key in the lock and put it in her pocket.

As her eyes became attuned to the gloom, she made out two gun belts within reach of the beds, hanging from a knob on the bed-heads. She managed to remove them both without undue disturbance, and tossed them through the open window on to the soft loam outside. Then she moved to the oil-lamp, and lit it from the box of lucifers alongside.

The sleeping men stirred slightly, but did not awaken. Deliberately she picked up a brush from the dressing-table nearby and slammed it on the floor.

Instantly both men jumped and struggled into wakefulness. First they looked at each other, then about them, and finally at the slim girl with a gun in each hand.

'You're going for a ride, boys,' she said briefly. 'Get dressed.'

'It's King's daughter,' Harral, the taller of the men exclaimed. His eyes moved to the empty bed-knob where his gun had been hanging. 'How in hell did she get in here?'

'Through the window,' Val said. 'Now get dressed!' She motioned with the guns threateningly. 'Don't be shy,' she added drily.

Having more sense than to try conclusions with a couple of guns, both men slid out of bed and drew on their outdoor clothes over their pyjamas, using the jackets as shirts. By the time they had finished and had their boots laced up several minutes had elapsed.

'Outside – through the window.' Val motioned to it with her right-hand gun. 'The door's locked.'

The men hesitated, then reluctantly obeyed as Val edged behind them.

'Keep your hands up,' she ordered. 'Go to your horses, wherever they are, and don't try anything. I won't hesitate to shoot – and you're also covered from outside.'

Both men moved across the yard to the dimness of the stables. Never for a moment did Val relax her vigilance. She kept the guns trained all the time while the men saddled their horses; then she made them lead the animals into the street by the side gate. When her father had been reached she called a halt.

'Get on your horses. We're riding out of here.'

'You're crazy if you think you can get away with this,' Lucas snapped.

'Shut up, and get mounted,' King said levelly, raising his gun at the speaker.

So the two punchers obeyed. Thereafter, as Val and her father swung into their own saddles, they had to keep riding through the slowly waxing light of dawn until the mountain foothills had been reached. Even then they were forced to ride higher until they reached a ledge with which Val was familiar.

'Dismount,' she ordered. 'Keep me covered, Dad, whilst I bind them up.'

'Go ahead, gal,' he responded, his left gun steady on the two men.

The men submitted as the girl got busy on them, twisting a lariat rope in and out of their ankles and carrying up to their wrists behind them, effectively hobbling them.

Satisfied they could not break free, Val looked at her father in the grey light.

'You have provisions enough to last for a while, Dad, together with bedrolls and other necessities. You stay here until I come and fetch you, when we're needed for the trial. We can leave these two turkeys nicely trussed up whilst you're away. Tied as they are now, they won't be able to try anything on you. Sure you'll be OK?'

King grinned. 'I reckon I can manage.'

'So that's your game! Keepin' us here away from the trial – you loco enough to think the sheriff will let you get away with this?' Harral demanded.

'Since neither the sheriff nor anyone else has any idea where you are – yes,' Val answered, with a grim smile. She turned to her father. 'I'd better get back to town, Dad, to see how things are developing.'

5

DESERT LAW

Absolutely sure of himself and unaware of what had happened in the night, Sheriff Crawford went to the mayor's office first thing in the morning and reported his indictment of Larry on a murder charge. The mayor, highly pleased with the news – having watched the start-tling metamorphosis of Larry from a safe distance – contacted Judge Gascoigne, to whom fell the task of presiding at all trials from cattle-thieving to murder which came within the orbit of Buzzard's Bend.

But Sheriff Crawford was a little too energetic. He only discovered after he had made all his statements that he couldn't locate his deputies. He went to their home in the main street, and, gaining no answer, used his authority to break in. Since the two men had lived together, with no other persons present, things were just as they had left them: bedclothes flung back, bedroom window open – and outside the window were the two gun belts with the guns in them.

Sheriff Crawford's immediate concern was to find the only two men who could back up the statements he had so freely made to the mayor, and subsequently to Judge Gascoigne. So he started searching and making enquiries with a band of his followers to help him – and failed to discover anything. Certainly it never occurred to him that Val and her father – a girl and a wounded man – had had anything to do with the business. All he could think of was some hitherto unknown friend or friends of Larry had stepped into the picture.

The two missing men were not found, and Crawford would have had much more sense to admit to the mayor and Judge Gascoigne that his two vital witnesses were missing; instead he clung to the belief that at the last minute they would turn up, and in consequence preparations for the trial went ahead.

In two more days it opened, and Sheriff Crawford was no nearer finding his witnesses on the morning he took his place in the stuffy courtroom, into which it seemed that every denizen of Buzzard's Bend had crammed. Judge Gascoigne, round-faced and genial, more like a favourite uncle than a dispenser of law, sat at his desk, his clerk immediately below him, whilst the picked jury of men and women waited for the proceedings to begin.

Morgan Granville, perhaps one shade less of a shyster than Makin had been, opened the proceedings for the prosecution, and Sheriff Crawford sat, sweating and glancing hopefully towards the doors of the courtroom. But the two men he wanted did not appear. He saw Val and her father enter as the trial commenced and take their seats near the front. They were not looking particularly troubled, and they smiled towards Larry as he stood in the railed enclosure doing service as a dock.

Then Morgan Granville, who talked with a powerful adenoidal strain, proceeded to explain to all and sundry how much of a two-cent heel Larry really was.

'And I contend,' he finished, after nearly twenty minutes of recounting details, 'that this man, Larry Ashfield, even though he be the nephew of the late respected Brian Ashfield, came amongst us under false colours. Pretending to be completely ineffectual, he led everybody to believe that he was a weakling, hoping no doubt to curry sympathy thereby, and perhaps cause the unfortunate Cliff Makin to reverse a legal clause, which, in all truth, he could not possibly do. In other words, when that man' – and Granville pointed accusingly towards Larry – 'knew that he would not be taking over a ranch and gold mine which he refused to believe was legally no longer his, he turned into a gun-happy madman. He made Cliff Makin his mortal enemy, and finally killed him. Not by a bullet, my friends, not by anything so clean as a knife – but by slamming his head against a wall until his neck was broken. That is the man who, I believe, should be found guilty of the foulest murder.'

Granville mopped his face and sat down. Then he began calling his witnesses. The Indian servant was the first; he explained how Makin had arrived, how high words had developed, how King had been shot through the hand, and how he – the servant – had considered it his duty to fetch the sheriff.

'In that capacity you acted rightly,' Judge Gascoigne said, adjusting his steel-rimmed glasses. 'But would it not have been simpler to rouse the men in the bunkhouse just across the yard? Surely they would have helped?'

'They not represent law, your honour,' the Indian answered. 'Mr King – he always tell me: fetch law if danger threaten. So I did.'

'Am I to understand, then, that the men in the bunkhouse had no idea of what was going on?' the judge asked.

'None,' the foreman of the Bar-6 said, standing up. 'It was late, and we had all gone to sleep, your honour.'

The judge nodded and relaxed in his chair. Granville gave the Indian a glance. 'You can stand down. Call Sheriff Crawford.'

The sheriff got up, mopping his face as he moved to the witness stand. Larry watched him curiously, quite unaware as yet of Val's strategy, it being against the law for them to converse with a man indicted for murder. Young William Gascoigne, son of the judge, and Larry's own defence lawyer, watched intently as Crawford took the oath.

'Now, Sheriff,' Granville said, considering him, 'I believe you have positive evidence of the fact that the prisoner murdered Cliff Makin?'

'Yes,' Crawford agreed; then uneasily, 'or at least I – I did have.'

Everybody looked at him sharply. William Gascoigne's eyes widened in sudden interest. His father adjusted his glasses.

'Did have?' Granville repeated. 'What exactly do you mean, Sheriff? You have the two deputies,' he paused and glanced at his notes – 'Lucas and Harral, who, with you, saw the murder committed, haven't you?'

'Er – no. They've disappeared. In fact, I haven't seen them since the night of the murder. . . .' Crawford turned appealingly to the judge. 'Your honour, that's the truth!

78

When I made my statement it was in good faith, and I was relying on my two deputies to corroborate me – as they would have done – but somebody is helping the prisoner, and the two witnesses I want have vanished.'

'Have you looked for them?' the judge asked quietly.

'Everywhere, but I can't trace them. My suggestion is that this trial be postponed to give me time to try and find them. I'm sure they can't be far away and—'

'That is a waste of the court's time,' Gascoigne interrupted. 'What other witnesses have you?'

'None,' Crawford muttered.

William Gascoigne sprang up.

'Your honour, this case has been brought by the prosecution without due regard to the facts! I can produce witnesses who can positively prove that the whole thing was an accident. Mr King and his daughter both saw what happened. I also have the statement of my own client and—'

'I would remind you, Mr Gascoigne, that *I* am still the judge,' his father said deliberately; then his gaze switched to the sheriff. 'Have you anything further to say, Sheriff, that can help to substantiate the charge you have brought?'

'How can I have without my witnesses?' Crawford demanded.

'But there must be something. . . .' Granville spread his hands helplessly, aware that the ground had been cut from under his feet.

The sheriff was silent. A murmur arose in the court, but the judge's gavel stopped it.

'Since no witnesses are being presented to support your charge, Sheriff, the case is dismissed. Free the prisoner.

And, Sheriff, I would like you to step into my room for a few minutes.'

That settled it. The courtroom became a sudden babel of conversation. Sheriff Crawford, following orders, got up from the witness's chair and trailed behind Judge Gascoigne to his chamber at the back of the courtroom. Larry, wasting no further time, vaulted the rail in front of him and hurried over to where Val and her father were standing.

'We did it,' Val said, kissing Larry in her sudden excitement. 'My idea worked!'

'Idea?' Larry kissed her in response and grinned.

'I arranged to get those two deputies out of the way,' Val explained, turning towards the exit. 'Right now they're up in the foothills. Dad's been watching them until I gave him the tip to turn up here as a witness. We never got as far as that, though.'

Behind the trio, as they stepped out into the bright sunlight, Hank – formerly Makin's henchman – glided away unnoticed, a glint in his pale eyes.

'You mean those two deputies are trussed up in the mountains?' Larry asked in surprise.

'Tied up good,' King conceded. 'I'm wondering just what we do with them now, unless you've any ideas, Larry?'

He nodded grimly. 'I've got plenty. I'll ride out with you and explain as we go. Wait for me whilst I reclaim my horse. I'll have to see Judge Gascoigne and get a release note for it. It's in the livery stable.'

Val and her father nodded, and went to their own horses, fastened to the tie rack beside the courthouse. It was ten minutes before Larry at last appeared, astride his own mount.

'Sorry for the delay,' he apologized. 'Old Gascoigne was wiping up the floor with Crawford for daring to bring a charge without being sure of substantiating it. I heard it even through the door. OK, let's go.'

He spurred his horse and followed Val and her father into the busy main street. In a matter of seconds they were through it and had hit the trail for the mountains.

'Just what have you in mind for Lucas and Harral?' King asked, as they sped along in the hot morning wind.

'Desert law,' Larry answered, his face grim. King glanced at the girl in surprise, then back to Larry's sternly set face.

'Surprised you know anything about that, son – being an Englishman, I mean.'

'I know all about it' Larry answered. 'My uncle was once a victim of it, and escaped. He wrote and told me about it. I also came across it again in those books I read from your shelf during my convalescence. In fact there's quite a lot I've learned about the West, after I'd decided to stop around these parts and fight for my rights.'

'And you think those two deputies of Crawford's should have the desert law invoked on them?' Val asked.

'It's logical,' Larry answered. 'According to the legal interpretation, any man in an official position – and that includes the deputies of a sheriff – who abuses it, either by perjury or any other cause, can be outlawed from the community. True, a committee of townsfolk usually perform the banishing ceremony, but in this case we can do it ourselves. Those two rats were fully prepared to confirm all of Crawford's lies and get me hanged. Instead, thanks to you two, the situation is reversed. I intend driving those men into the desert. They can then either

81

struggle to the next town, or die. It doesn't matter which.'

'Sounds to me,' King said presently, 'as though you've sure got the hang of this territory very nicely, son.'

'Kill or be killed seems to be the watchword,' Larry said. 'I'm living by it.'

He said no more until the foothills were reached, and eventually the ledge upon which lay the two deputies, still firmly bound, in the midst of the camp King had made. They glared up at Larry as he advanced towards them.

'So you got free?' Lucas sneered. 'Was it legal or did you make a dash fur it?'

'It was legal – same as what I've planned for you.' Larry turned to Val as she came up. 'Let me have one of your guns and a belt, Val. I'm without.'

She nodded and handed them over. Larry strapped the belt about his waist and held the gun in his hand.

'All right, Val – release them,' he said. 'I'm covering you.'

She unfastened the ropes, and the two men slowly got to their feet, rubbing their numbed arms and legs. Larry gave them time to recover, and then eyed them fixedly.

'You two are riding into the desert yonder. You'll be allowed to ride half-way, then you'll be given a water bottle each. After that it will be up to you whether you can make the next nearest town on foot – or rot on the way.'

'You mean desert law?' Harral demanded, appalled. 'What are we supposed to have done that—'

'You both sold yourselves as liars to Crawford, and that's enough for me. Further, I'm not taking the chance of your going back into Buzzard's Bend to start telling your lies about what really happened. It might not affect me – but, on the other hand, it could. So you're leaving here, and if you ever show your faces anywhere in this territory again, you can be shot dead. That's part of the law, too. Even if nobody else does the shooting, I will. Now get on your horses.'

Larry nodded to them as they stood sleepily in the shade of the mountain face, their horses reined to a rock spur. The two men looked at each other helplessly, then at the gun in Larry's hand. They untied their horses and eased themselves painfully into the saddles, as Larry, Val and King also remounted.

'Get going,' Larry ordered. 'I'm right behind you. If you carry on along this ledge, it should dip further on and lead into a pass. After that there's the open desert.' Catching Val's surprised glance, he added: 'There were two maps of this district pinned up in the sheriff's office within sight of my cell. I spent a lot of the time in jail studying them. Now it's coming in useful.'

Larry was right, for the ledge did at length dip down into a declivity and thereafter into a pass. Beyond the pass the whole vast expanse of the desert lay ahead, shimmering and yellow in the blazing midday sun. On the remote horizon a purple smudge denoted the approximate position of Prescott, the nearest town.

Thereafter the party only paused at water holes, during which periods the men said nothing as they sat on their sweating beasts. Then on again, until, after one pause for some food, Larry adjudged the half-way mark had been reached and called a halt.

The whole world seemed to be made up of endless sand, scorching-hot even through riding-boots, and the relentless sun in the cloudless cobalt of the sky.

Larry motioned to the two men to dismount, then

pointed to the smudge on the horizon.

'Somewhere over there lies Prescott. You can make it, or pass out trying. Here's a water bottle each.'

He hande over two bottles – one of his own and one of King's, having ascertained that on Val's horse there was ample water supply in a small drum.

'Now move,' Larry ordered, his gun levelled. 'And keep on going!'

Sullenly the two men turned away, shambling through the sand, wiping their faces with the backs of their hands as they went. Larry stood watching them go for a while, then turned to look at the serious faces of Val and her father.

'Maybe tough justice,' he said, 'but it's not murder – as they as good as planned that for me. And I'm pretty sure those two were in the bunch of men who tried to roast me alive on the hillside. At least they've a chance of reaching safety. I had none. All right, we'll take their horses and hit the trail for home. Come on.'

He moved to his horse and then paused, squinting into the shimmering heat waves of the distance. Far away as yet were several approaching riders, and obviously moving fast, to judge from rate at which they increased in size.

'Looks like trouble coming, son,' King said. 'What do we do, Larry?'

'Wait and see who it is,' he answered. 'Meantime we'd better get down behind this dune in case there's any shooting. Grab the horses.'

He reined his own horse, and those of the two punchers, and pulled them swiftly into the comparative protection of the dune nearby. King and Val did likewise, then all three of them lay in the blazingly hot sand and peered over the rim, grains blowing irritatingly into their eyes.

They knew that they had almost certainly been seen. The one thing they hoped for was that if there was any shooting they would at least stand a chance with the dune to protect them. Just how the position stood they soon realized as the horsemen came within range and started pumping lead for all they were worth. Along the top of the dune sand spat into the air as bullets plugged it.

'It's that skunk, Hank,' Larry whispered, the hammer cocked on his borrowed gun. 'Him and about a dozen other guys – and Sheriff Crawford too! The whole damned bunch of 'em must have followed us, somehow.'

'Maybe I talked too freely back in the courthouse,' Val said contritely. 'I was so excited I didn't quite realize how many people were around us. *Oh*!' She started back as a bullet exploded sand not a fraction from her right hand.

The nearness of the shot brought a glint into her eyes as she snatched out her remaining gun and cocked it. She wriggled her way slightly upwards until she could just see over the rim of the dune without revealing herself. The horsemen had drawn up a short distance away, evidently not venturing closer to the dune for fear of drawing too many bullets at their higher angle.

Val sighted quickly – and fired. One of the men threw up his hands and dropped from his saddle into the sand.

'Nice shooting, gal,' King grunted, but his voice was troubled. 'We're outnumbered four to one, and this dune is wide enough for them to come round the back of it. They can riddle us if we aren't careful.'

'Not if we riddle them first,' Larry said. 'That's our only chance. Give them everything we've got!'

He squirmed his way up the sandy slope once more

and, risking any bullets that might come his way, he fired three times in quick succession. One of his bullets missed, but the other two brought down another couple of men. Only one lay unmoving; the other picked himself up, clutching his shoulder.

'*Look out!*' King cried suddenly, and just in time Larry saw that two men were on the edge of the dune, about to leap down upon him – the two men he had sent into the desert.

Many things abruptly became clear to him. The two men, recognizing friends, had returned – which accounted for the others holding their fire. A sudden leap down on the trio could easily have gained them an advantage – but Larry acted in the split seconds he had to observe them.

He fired savagely, twice in quick succession. Lucas, the right-hand man, buckled at the knees and collapsed in the sand. His companion, Harral, clawed the air, wheeled round, and then crashed headlong down the dune and became motionless.

'That does it,' King said grimly. 'They won't hold their fire up there any longer. Be ready for anything.'

But it seemed he was wrong. No bullets came.

'Anyway,' Larry said, looking up from a quick examination of the two men he had shot, 'these two will never give any fake evidence now, and—'

'*Get your hands up – the lot of you!*'

Larry twisted and fired savagely. His bullet went wide. The second time his hammer clicked on emptiness, the chambers exhausted. He put the weapon in its holster and stared fixedly at Sheriff Crawford and Hank, standing a foot or two away. They had done the thing King had feared

– sneaked up from behind. But, strangely, they did not seem in any particular hurry to use their guns.

Holding them but not firing them, they came forward to where the trio now kneeled in the sand, their hands raised. King had his uninjured left arm up, which was the best he could do.

'Take their guns, Hank,' Crawford said briefly, and when it had been done he surveyed the three and grinned coldly.

'Mebbe we can get better results out here than leavin' it to a legal-minded dimwit like Judge Gascoigne,' he said. 'Thanks to you snatchin' my two boys, I got censured by that fool judge and you, Ashfield, escaped a necktie party. I also notice that you've plugged my deputies over there – but even if I can't pin the Makin rap on you now, mebbe I can exercise a little justice on my own account.'

'Come to the point, can't you?' King snapped. 'Why don't you shoot that damned gun and get it over with?'

'A quick death with a bullet in the heart is too good for what you've done,' Crawford explained venomously. 'And anyway, bullets are too easy to trace. Besides, I'm thinking of making you smart a bit before you die.'

'I always did think you were a sadist, Crawford,' Val commented bitterly. But there was no fear in her voice. 'What are you planning to do with us?'

'Nothing much – I'm just going to bury you in the sand and leave it at that.'

'You mean – bury us alive?' King demanded incredulously.

'Not quite.' The sheriff grinned sadistically. 'I just aim to have you buried as far as your necks. I reckon the sun and sand'll do the rest. Down in this dune here nobody'll ever see you if they come ridin' this desert trail, and you sure won't see them. OK, boys,' he called, raising his voice. 'Fetch three lariats.'

Presently several of the men returned, carrying thin, tough ropes. Crawford motioned with his gun.

'Tie up these three separately – and make it good. You other boys can start digging three holes, deep enough to take each of these three as high as their chins.'

'What about our own casualties?' one of the men asked. 'Are you just leavin' them here for the buzzards?'

'We're taking their bodies back to town for burial, you bonehead!' Crawford snapped impatiently. 'We've no time for anything else. It's hot enough out here to a burn the damned brains outa a man. Hurry it up, and get those three holes dug.'

Having no implements with them, the men had to use their hands, but the sand being fairly soft it did not take them very long to burrow down. Tightly bound, not speaking, Larry, Val, and her father looked at the three holes and then at each other.

'Mighty nice,' Hank said, with a glance at Crawford. 'I couldn't have thought of anythin' better myself.'

'Dump 'em in – and pack the sand tight,' Crawford snapped. 'Hurry it up!'

Larry was the first to be lifted and lowered into the hole assigned for him. Sand was poured in around him and packed tight. At last it had risen to chin level, and he was left with his head protruding from the sand.

'Take his hat away,' Crawford growled. 'He don't need that – and neither does King or the girl. Blast it, hurry up!' he yelled, as the men hesitated. 'We're not durned well frying here much longer than we can help!'

It seemed pretty obvious that some of the men were not such hardened brutes as Crawford, but he had the guns and the authority, so they did as they were told. Val was the next to be buried to chin level; then came her father, no regard for his tightly bound, injured hand being shown.

'Yeah, very pretty,' Crawford said eventually, wiping the streaming perspiration from his face. 'That'll teach you to play games with me. OK, boys, let's go. Take their horses with us. . . .'

'Reckon we can't do that,' Hank said, looking about him. 'They've gone. Musta stampeded when all those shots were fired. Couldn't have been hitched to anything.'

'Find 'em,' Crawford ordered. 'Horseflesh is mighty valuable.'

With a shrug Joe toiled to the top of the dune, mopping his face. The hot wind smote him as he came to the desert level. Far away, and apparently becoming remoter, were three black specks. He gave a grunt of disgust and turned.

'Durned things are on the run, miles away,' he said. 'I don't fancy chasin' after them in this heat, Sheriff.'

'OK, leave 'em,' Crawford said. 'Let's hit leather for somewheres less hot.'

He gave one more malign glance at the buried trio and then, with his men, scrambled up the sandbank and disappeared from sight. There was the faint, distant thunder of hoofs – and then silence. To the three buried in the sand it felt as though their faces were close to molten lead whilst their bodies, cramped with ropes and packed with sand, were feeling deadly cold and numb.

'Be a couple of hours until this sun begins to sink,' Val said, squinting up into the glare. 'Until then I suppose we just fry. I always knew Sheriff Crawford had no scruples, but I didn't think he'd ever stoop to this.'

She made a useless effort to try and release the ropes pinning her arms and legs. The tightly jamming sand prevented the slightest movement. All she could do, like her father and Larry, was stand motionless and feel the life being slowly numbed from her body whilst the heat seared her head and face.

'How long,' King said presently, licking his cracked lips, 'd'you suppose we can hold out?'

'Depends on our constitutions,' Larry muttered, with an anxious glance at Val. He noticed that her head was now lolling backwards on the sand, her eyes closed to the intolerable glare. Perspiration gleamed like a film over her strained features.

Time passed with agonizing slowness. As a form of torture it was exquisite.

'Say,' King whispered, his voice hoarse, 'what d'you reckon that is, Larry? Over to your right. . . .'

Larry turned his head with an effort and then frowned. A dark, peculiarly shaped moving shadow was being cast on the sand from behind the ridge of the dune. Both Larry and King were still trying to work it out when there was a sudden whinny in the still-sizzling air.

'One of our horses!' King gasped. 'I'd forgotten 'em. They've come back. Here, boy,' he broke off, clicking his teeth, 'come here. . . .'

There was another whinny, which this time seemed to have a touch of delight in it, and the shadow moved quickly. One of the three horses loomed into view and stood, looking into the gully, kneading sand with his forelegs.

'It's Blackie, my own sorrel,' King gasped. 'Here,

Blackie – good boy. Come here.'

Blackie came down into the gully obediently and stood a few feet away as though trying to decide what to do next.

'We've one chance,' Larry said urgently. 'I can do it better than you because I'm uninjured and lighter than you are. If I can only get those dangling reins under my chin, Blackie might pull me free! After that I can roll to you and you can unpick my rope knots with your teeth.'

'It's a chance,' King agreed, without hesitation. 'Go for it, son.'

Larry tried calling the horse to him. It showed the whites of its eyes, snorted and sweated, and remained motionless. There was an added danger at this moment. The blazing heat might easily cause it to lose control of itself. If it did that and its hoofs lashed out at the heads at ground level. . . !

'Blackie,' Larry called gently, fighting hard against dizziness. 'Come here, boy. That's it,' he murmured, as the animal at last came towards him. 'Nearer. . . Good lad. Nearer. . . .'

The horse did not understand, and it kept shambling about in a half-circle, the loop of the reins dangling about a foot from Larry's head as he struggled to stretch his chin near them.

'No use,' he groaned. 'The dumb beast just doesn't get the idea . . . but he's *got* to!' he added fiercely. 'Look at Val there. She's been lying like that for nearly fifteen minutes – the sun beating into her face. Blackie, damn you, come here!'

The animal moved, stopped in front of Larry, and snorted.

'I've got it!' King said abruptly. 'If I call him he might

91

step over you to come to me – give you a chance to get the reins under your chin. But for God's sake mind you don't get strangled!'

'Strangled or fried, what's the difference?' Larry growled. 'Try it!'

King clicked his teeth. 'Here, Blackie,' he called. Good boy! Here. . . .'

Blackie moved, stepping neatly over Larry's head. He angled his chin quickly and the leather loop caught beneath it.

'Call him again!' he gasped. 'Quick!'

Desperately, King did so. Realizing he was being dragged downwards at the bit, Blackie set his back legs and lurched forward to his master. To Larry it felt as though his jaw was being crushed as his body was dragged from the sand piled around him. He came out as far as his knees and then lay on his face, gasping, the reins swinging free again.

'So far, so good,' he panted, and began to roll over until he had reached King's side.

As the horse blew through its nostrils and kneaded its legs impatiently, King had all the work to do. His strong teeth bit and tugged at the knots about Larry's wrists, his task made tougher by the fact that dampness in the sand had tightened the fibres. The heat was all on the surface: a foot below it was cold.

'OK,' King breathed at last, oblivious to his bleeding gums. 'Try pulling your wrists free now, Larry.' He relaxed, panting hard.

Larry tugged furiously at his wrists and they came apart. After that it did not take him long to free the rest of his body. Immediately he dived across to Val and began to scoop the sand from about her. Lifting her slack body in his arms, he carried her to the further end of the gully, where the slowly descending sun had created a lengthening shadow. She stirred slightly as Larry tore the ropes away from her.

Leaving her to recover consciousness, he returned to King and dug him out. The old man was utterly exhausted but otherwise unhurt. Trailing Blackie beside him, he staggered across with him into the shadowy area. A word from him brought the horse down on its knees, then on its side, so that it was out of the sunlight.

'How's things, Val?' Larry murmured, slipping his arm behind her shoulders as she stirred into wakefulness.

She did not answer as she passed a hand over her damp forehead and breathed hard. King gave her a glance and then looked around him.

'Wonder what happened to the other two cayuses?' he asked. 'Guess I might take a look. . . .'

He struggled painfully to his feet and went up the dune, thankful for the hot wind that fanned his sun-cracked face as he reached the top of the rise. Almost immediately he discerned two black shapes moving aimlessly not very far away.

'Here, boys,' he shouted. 'Gee-up! Here. . . .'

Attracted by his familiar voice, the horses turned and began to trot towards him. In another few moments they had arrived. He caught at their reins and led them down into the gully, forced them to lie down, and then unfastened the water barrel from the back of Val's horse.

'Here, son – give the gal some water,' he said, rejoining Larry and handing the barrel over. Larry took it from him carefully, and held it steadily as Val drank some of the warm liquid. At last she relaxed and covered her face with her hands.

'What goes on?' King asked in surprise. 'She's OK, isn't she?'

'The sun's got her,' Larry answered grimly 'She's got a tearing headache and she can't see.'

'*What?*' King stared blankly, then he caught Val in his arms and looked down into her face. She opened her eyes and blinked at him.

'Don't start worrying about me, Dad,' she said huskily. 'I – I guess I'll be OK when I – I get rid of this headache. It's pretty nearly – killing me!'

She beat the sand with her fists and twisted her body helplessly in a vain effort to escape the anguish that gripped her. King took her in his arms again and held her tightly.

'Take it easy, youngster,' he murmured, kissing her forehead. 'We'll see that you'll be OK. It's just a touch of the sun. I've nursed you better before, after I lost your dear mother, and I can do it again.'

She squirmed a little in his grip. 'Dad, it's no use,' she whispered. 'I'm blind! Don't you realize that? Everything's black.'

'Yeah,' King said gently. 'Sure it is. Sun-blindness happens in the desert many a time. Had it myself. Fair blows your brains apart while it lasts. You'll be OK when the night comes.'

He exchanged a grim look with Larry, who got on his feet and wiped his face.

'Crawford's got plenty to answer for,' he said tautly. 'Time we were riding back into town. Are you taking Val or shall I? We can shade her from the sun with our bodies.'

94

'I'll take her,' King decided. 'She's my kid. I know how to handle her.'

Larry nodded and turned to the horses. He and King then both took a drink – not too much – then King climbed into his saddle and took the softly moaning girl into his lap as Larry gently raised her up. His face as hard as granite, Larry mounted his own horse, taking Val's in tow, and then led the way up the slope.

Then they were riding through the searing waste, the shadows lengthening about them. But they still had a considerable distance to go before they escaped from the wilderness.

6

DUEL OF DEATH

The edge of the desert was not reached until nightfall, and here Larry called for their third halt, stopping at the first water hole on the trail that led across country to Buzzard's Bend.

Val, who seemed to have recovered slightly with the coming of the night, was lifted down by Larry and laid so that her head and shoulders were propped by rockery. He held the water barrel for her whilst she drank.

'Any better, Val?' Larry murmured.

'I guess so.' Her voice was weak. 'At least I don't feel as if my head's about to fall off any more. But I still can't see anything.'

'Not much to see if you could.' Larry sat alongside, his arm around her. 'Night's come. There's only the stars and. . . .' He paused, so abruptly that he felt the girl tense in his grip.

'What is it?' she asked quickly.

'I dunno . . ' Larry turned to where King was half-lying

beside him, grateful for the brief rest. 'Say, Mr King, what do you suppose that glow is over there? Flickering in the distance?'

'Fire of some sort, I reckon.'

'Doesn't it occur to you it's in the same direction as the Bar-6?'

'Huh?' King scrambled to his feet and watched the distant flickering intently. 'Sweet juniper, you're right,' he breathed. 'Don't tell me that two-bit sheriff has set fire to our spread!'

'Sooner we ride out and see the better,' Larry said, helping Val to her feet. 'The horses have had their drink at the water hole, so let's move. Hang on to me, Val, you'll be OK.'

Larry guided her into the saddle of his horse. Then he was behind her almost immediately and started the horse forward. Behind him, trailing Val's horse, King followed quickly.

Tired though the animals were, Larry did not spare the pace. He kept his eyes on the distant glow as he thundered his horse along the night trail, Val clinging tightly to him. She could not bring herself to say anything. The blindness afflicting her made her begin to fear that perhaps she would never again see the beauty of the country in which she had been raised.

Gradually, lulled by the rocking motion of the horse, and having nothing but blackness around her, she fell asleep. She only awoke again as Larry's voice immediately above startled her.

'It's the Bar-6 all right. Come on!'

He goaded his horse forward down the long slope of pastureland that led to the Bar-6, King thundering behind him. Both men could see now see that the ranch house itself seemed as yet untouched, but the barns were afire and several of the outhouses. At the yard gate Larry dismounted swiftly and lowered Val to her feet. He put her fingers in contact with the saddle.

'Wait here a moment, Val,' he said briefly. 'I'll come back and get you.'

'Yes – all right,' she assented, and listened intently. She heard her father speed past her, and could also hear the shouts of men and the crackle of flames. Furiously she blinked her eyelids, savage with herself that she was quite unable to see anything – then Larry's footsteps came back and his arm encircled her waist.

'Things are OK,' he said. 'The ranch was fired at the same time as the outhouses and barns, but the boys put it out in time. They've also got the other half of the fire under control now. They don't know who did it, but I can make a pretty good guess.'

'Where's Dad?' Val asked anxiously.

'Taking stock of what's been lost. He's sent one of the boys into town to fetch Doc Barnes to see you. Let's be moving.'

Val felt herself lifted from her feet and she was carried to the ranch house. She could sense its walls about her, and presently found herself sprawling in the soft comfort of her bed. A lucifer scraped, but she did not see the flame.

'Larry . . .' she whispered. 'You and Dad seem to be taking everything so casually in regard to my sight. Do you suppose that I might never. . . .'

'Don't worry,' Larry said gently, patting her arm. 'You'll be OK, just as your dad promised. Just relax. I'll bring you something to eat and drink; then I'll get that squaw servant of yours to examine you for bruises.'

Val relaxed, her hands to her throbbing eyes. At least the last traces of her violent headache seemed to have gone. She could think clearly, and, save for her tiredness, felt almost bodily fit. Except for. . .

'I don't believe it,' she whispered. 'Not that! It just couldn't happen to me. To be in the dark for the rest of my life after all the things we've. . . .'

She turned her face into the pillow and cried, only relaxing as she felt Larry's hand gently drawing at her shoulder.

'Easy does it, Val,' he whispered. 'Here, sit up. I've brought you something to eat and drink.'

He was glad she could not see his expression as she drank the coffee he put into her hand. Her father came into the bedroom, moving silently as he studied her.

'About time Doc Barnes showed up,' he said grimly.

'Hardly time yet,' Larry said.

'Dad, tell me the truth!' Val turned toward the sound of his voice. 'How badly damaged do you suppose my eyes are? You told me out in the desert you'd had the same thing, and that it passed off.'

'Yeah – sure thing.' King gave Harry a grim look. 'It'll do the same with you . . . Only thing you can do right now is finish your meal and then get to bed properly. Doc Barnes will be here soon. I'll send in—'

'You needn't bother, Dad. I'm not so incapable I can't get undressed. Maybe I'd better begin getting used to it. . . .' She pushed away the food that she felt at her hand. 'Just leave me alone,' she pleaded.

Larry jerked his head and followed King into the living-room. King closed the door and came over to the table, his face grim.

'I've got all the facts now about the fire,' he said. 'Little doubt it was done by Sheriff Crawford and his boys. Not satisfied with leaving us to die, they also tried to burn down our spread and stampede the cattle. If my men in the bunkhouse hadn't been running a late-night card-school, they'd have gotten away with it, too.'

'But why did he fire the ranch?' Larry asked coldly.

'I think I know,' King said slowly. 'Even had we died, as Crawford figured, my foreman would have carried on with the ranch in my place. Some time ago I gave him the legal right to do that if anything ever happened to me and Val. Crawford, since he was thick with Makin – with whom I had the deed prepared – would know that. In other words, he didn't want opposition from this thriving ranch because he's also in cahoots with Simon Gait at the Double-L. It all fits, Larry. The sheriff knew Makin well; Simon Gait knew both men. Between them – the mayor thrown in – I fancy they are making a pile out of the gold mine attached to the Double-L, to say nothing of the cattle on the ranch itself. Wiping out my spread would have killed a good deal of rival trading. . . .' He sat down heavily at the table, nursing his arm.

'I'm going to get Crawford,' Larry said, his eyes hard in the lamplight. 'And if Val has been permanently blinded because of him, I'm going to put his eyes out in return – slowly. With a cigarette end, maybe. I'll make him squirm. . . .'

Larry stopped, controlling himself as there were sounds in the hall. Doc Barnes, not looking very pleased at the lateness of the call-out, came into the room.

'What this time?' he asked, dumping his bag on the table. 'Your man just said it was urgent.'

'It's Val, Doc.' King got to his feet again. 'Something wrong with her eyes. We – were out in the sun longer than we should have been.'

'Oughta have more sense,' Barnes growled, as King opened Val's bedroom door and then closed it again after him.

Larry lighted a cigarette and drew at it viciously, a cruel twist in the line of his jaw. King drank two whiskeys and then mooched about the big room, unable to think of anything to say. It seemed that Barnes was taking an interminable time. When he emerged again it was fifteen minutes past midnight.

'You're a bright-looking pair of critters,' he said frankly, snapping the catches shut on his bag. 'Get some sleep – you look as if you need it.'

'What about Val?' Larry asked deliberately. 'Is she going to be—'

'You can both stop worrying.' Barnes gave a sympathetic smile for a moment. 'She'll be all right. Just sunblindness. If she weren't the darned healthy kid she is, it might have been permanent – but all the reactions are there. That headache she had probably helped to save her eyes. It worked like a kind of safety valve. In a couple of days she'll be able to spot a coyote a mile away.'

'Thank God for that,' King whispered, all tiredness forgotten.

'One thing I don't get,' Barnes said. 'She's got a sunburn fit to fry eggs on – and you two guys are pretty well blistered as well. How in hell did all this *happen*?'

'We were dry-gulched,' King said bitterly. 'One thing,

Doc: don't tell a soul that we're here and alive. I don't want our enemies alerted and mebbe striking again before we can act.'

'OK. I don't know anything,' Barnes promised. 'As for Val, she must stay with that bandage round her eyes for a couple of days, then she can take it off and see what happens. If nothing does, better send for me again, but unless I studied medicine for nothing you'll not need to bother. 'Night to you both.'

After the doctor had left King and Larry stood looking at each other. Then with one accord they hurried to Val's room. As they entered they slowed up and smiled ruefully. Val lay still, her eyes bandaged and her breathing regular. The girl was fast asleep. On the table the oil-lamp still burned.

'That's one fine girl you raised, sir,' Larry murmured. He tiptoed to the lamp and turned it out. Both men silently withdrew, closing the door carefully behind them.

Back in the living-room, King stifled a yawn. 'We need to hit the hay to recover our strength. After that, what's the programme? You still going to blind Crawford?'

'No, I guess he's escaped that,' Larry answered, thinking. 'But he'll certainly pay for what he's done. It seems to me now that only two men are standing in my way and preventing me getting the Double-L and the mine. One is Crawford and the other is Simon Galt. I haven't had the chance to meet him so far – been too busy dealing with Makin. What sort of man is he?'

'We haven't had any supper,' King said as if it had just dawned on him. 'I guess we can stay up long enough to have a bite to eat. It'll give me a chance to tell you what I know of Simon Galt.'

Larry nodded as King turned and went looking in the kitchen, not wanting to rouse the Indian servant and his wife. In a few minutes he and King were busy with a meal of reheated stew, and a large coffee jug.

'Galt's a greasy customer,' King explained. 'I've only met him twice. He's an oddity out here because he's a teetotaller – that's one reason why you've never seen him in the Lucky Dollar. He has little need to come into town, since he can control everything from the Double-L.'

'Where did he blow in from originally?' Larry asked.

'No idea – somewhere East. Next thing we heard, through the *Buzzard's Bend Times*, was that he had bought the Double-L and the gold mine through Makin.'

'According to Makin, my uncle owed Galt a lot of money, and the ranch and gold mine were in part-payment.' Larry drank some coffee. 'I'm pretty sure that story is trumped up. . . .'

'Knowing Makin, I agree with you, son.'

'In Makin's office there ought to be some evidence somewhere to prove just how he stole the Double-L and the mine from me,' Larry continued. 'The sort of evidence that a marshal might find interesting, since he can override the local authority. If I could find such evidence I'd turn it in to the authorities in Prescott and get them to send a law officer here to look into matters.'

'Yeah.' King considered this as he chewed steadily. 'But examining Makin's office wouldn't be so easy. You can be sure that Crawford will have it covered from every angle. There must be plenty in that office that can put Crawford in a tough spot too. Unless he's already used his authority as sheriff to open up the office and remove anything that incriminates him.'

'Possible,' Larry admitted, thinking. 'On the other hand, Crawford may know who will take over Makin's practice when all the details are settled, and it may not matter whether this newcomer knows all about Crawford. In fact, that is the probable answer. I can't see Crawford, as Makin's best friend and sheriff of the town, allowing anybody to buy the practice unless he be one of his own flock of two-timers.'

'Yeah – like Morgan Granville, mebbe. That guy struck me as a shyster, the way he tried to twist the evidence against you in court. But where does that get us?'

'I'm going to shoot it out with Sheriff Crawford,' Larry said deliberately. 'Tomorrow evening, before witnesses, I'm going to accuse him of attempted murder – meaning ourselves and Val. If he shoots me, that ends it; if it's the other way around, I'm going to try and take his place as sheriff. That will give me the chance to wipe the floor with this gang of crooks who've fouled Buzzard's Bend for long enough.'

'Crawford's mighty useful with a gun,' King said, frowning.

'So am I.' Larry got to his feet. 'And it was Val who taught me.'

Throughout the next day Larry spent his time with Val. She was up and about as usual, apparently recovered from the ordeal in the desert except for her eyes. With them bandaged she had to feel her way about, or else be led – but it did not dampen her spirits. The assurances of Doc Barnes the night before had convinced her that her prison door would soon be open.

During the day Larry took good care that he, King and

Val remained indoors, and all members of the outfit had been warned not to reveal that the ranch house was occupied. That the Bar-6 had not been burned down was something of which Crawford must have been aware, but it did not particularly signify. And during the morning Larry dispatched one of the boys to town to purchase a couple of new .45s. When they were brought he spent the time, during the afternoon, trying them out in the one remaining ungutted outhouse, getting the feel of the weapons, Val seated nearby and listening to the impact of the bullets on an old frying-pan.

'You seem to have got the hang of them, Larry,' she said at last, as his arm came about her shoulder.

'Just as well,' he responded. 'I'm going to need it for tonight's shoot-out.'

'Just how do you mean – shoot-out?' Val asked.

'Don't you know? You've lived around here all your life, Val.' Larry took the girl's arm and walked her gently across the rear of the yard to the back entrance of the ranch house. 'To shoot it out is quite legitimate. I read of it in those books of your dad's when I was convalescent.'

'I must read them sometime.' Val hesitated. 'That is, I will if I. . . .'

'Don't bring that up again,' Larry said severely. 'You're going to be fine. As I was saying, shooting it out is about the same as a duel. You accuse your opponent of something and challenge him to shoot it out. If he refuses he's stamped as a coward, so naturally he agrees. The people around are witnesses. There are so many paces – turn and fire. One or the other – sometimes both – gets the slug where it hurts most. If one dies it isn't murder because each party has agreed to take the risk of dying.'

'But, Larry, that means you might lose.' Val seized his arm more tightly. 'I'm sure there ought to be some other way of tackling things without risking your life.'

'There isn't, Val, and you know it! In this region you live or die by the gun: that's one lesson I've learned well. I believe in justice enough to feel sure that I shan't be allowed to die and a man like Crawford to live.'

Val did not attempt to argue any more, knowing it was useless. It made it even harder for her when she had to stay behind at the ranch that evening with her father whilst Larry set off at nightfall. She wondered if he would ever return.

Half an hour after he had departed she suddenly got to her feet from the chair beside the fireplace, and began fiddling with the bandage around her head.

'Hold it, gal! What are you doing?' her father demanded.

'Taking this beastly thing off! I can't stand it any longer! I've got to know whether I can see yet or not. If I can I'm going after Larry to watch what happens. If otherwise . . But I've *got* to see!' she finished desperately.

'Wait! Doc Barnes said two days, and. . .'

With a sudden wrench she had the bandage free and stood with her eyelids closed, her hand gripping the table. She slowly opened her eyes. The first thing she saw was the seemingly dazzlingly bright light of the oil-lamp. It sent twinges deep into her eyes, and then abated. Breathless, she looked at her father's fixed expression, at the fire, the familiar room.

'Dad!' she cried hoarsely. 'Doc Barnes was right! I can see again!'

She plunged forwards on to her knees and his arms

gripped her shoulders gently. He took no notice of her sudden tears of relief.

'Just as well, gal,' he murmured. 'That story I spun you about having had the same experience myself was just a lot of moonshine, to cheer you up.'

'You old twister, you,' she said, looking up with a rueful smile and dabbing at her tears with her handkerchief. Then she got quickly on her feet. 'I'm following Larry,' she said, speeding into her room for her mackinaw. 'Are you coming with me?'

'You bet I am!'

Meanwhile Larry had just reached town. He tied his horse's reins to the rack outside the Lucky Dollar, and then went up the steps to the batwings. With a deliberate movement, he pushed them aside and, his new guns swinging low from his thighs, walked across to the bar counter.

'Whiskey,' he ordered, and surveyed the smoky room with its crowd of customers. It was not long before his gaze settled on Sheriff Crawford, paunchy and complacent, yarning with Hank and another puncher at a nearby table.

Larry drank off his whiskey, refilled the glass, and then met Crawford's gaze across distance. Crawford stared fixedly, took a quick drink, and looked again. He turned to Hank. He gazed too – and so did the third puncher. The noise of the saloon continued, regardless of the cold hate with which the three men measured each other.

'Folks, your attention, please!' Larry called suddenly, as he saw the mayor was not far away either.

The murmuring of voices faded as Larry banged the

bar counter with his gun butt. When complete silence had fallen he spoke again.

'I suppose most of you here know what it means to shoot it out with a man, so I'm telling you that's what I'm proposing to do. The man I'm challenging is Sheriff Crawford. The charge I make against him is attempted murder – with torture thrown in.'

Crawford got to his feet, his face black with fury.

'How the hell dare you make a charge like that when you can't prove it?' he demanded.

'Get wise to the law of shooting it out, Sheriff,' Larry retorted. 'I don't need to prove anything. This isn't a trial: it's an accusation. You left Val King, her father, and me to die in the desert, buried to our necks in the sand. How we got away is none of your business, but because of it Val King is blind. On top of that you tried to set fire to the Bar-6. I'm challenging you to shoot it out with me, Crawford. If I win, it's justice: if I don't – well, it's my funeral.'

'It's all a lot of dirty lies!' Crawford shouted, striding over to the bar. How much of the tale was true, nobody could say . . . until Doc Barnes rose from a quiet corner.

'Not quite, Crawford. Late last night, folks, I was called to the Bar-6 to treat Val King for sun-blindness, and I also know that her father, and Mr Ashfield here were severely sunburned and clearly exhausted. They spoke of enemies who had bushwhacked them, but they gave no names.'

'I bet they didn't,' Crawford sneered. 'Now they're trying to pin it on me!'

'There's nobody else to pin it on,' Larry said levelly. 'Are you shooting it out, or are you scared?'

'Scared!' Crawford laughed shortly. 'If you want to be rubbed out, fella, I'll oblige you!'

'Right,' Larry agreed. 'That's settled. Better clear a space, folks. . . .'

He paused and looked up. He could hardly credit it as he saw Val hurrying through the batwings and heading towards him between the tables, her father following behind.

'Larry!' she cried, seizing his arm. 'Thank heaven I'm in time. I can't let you take such a risk.'

'But what's happened? You can see again!'

'Yes. I tried it out at home – and came straight here when I found I was all right.'

'Look here, Ashfield, what kind of tale are you trying to hand me?' Crawford demanded. 'This girl is clearly unharmed, and you—'

'Miss King has recovered in the normal way of things,' Barnes said, coming forward. 'Ashfield spoke the truth about her, Sheriff. I can vouch for that.'

'And my accusation stands,' Larry said. 'I'm ready when you are, Sheriff. Stand aside, Val – I'm going through with this.' He signalled to King to draw the girl away. The old man did so.

Within a few moments all the tables in the centre of the floor had been cleared, and Doc Barnes was called upon to conduct the proceedings. Knowing the meaning of 'shooting it out,' he was meticulously exact. Larry and Crawford each drew their left guns and tossed them to one side. The right ones they left in the holsters.

'You will each take twelve paces, keeping time with my counting,' Barnes instructed. 'On the count of twelve you will draw, turn, and shoot. Ready?'

Both men nodded, and Barnes began counting.

'One, two, three, four—'

'*Look out!*' Val screamed.

Larry swung, drew, and fired. A bullet whined past his ear and splintered a back-bar mirror. Crawford, who had turned eight paces too soon, stood rocking on his feet, red staining his shirt over the heart. He lurched, his smoking gun dropping from his fingers; then he crashed face down into the sawdust.

Silence. Larry stood with cordite fumes curling round his nostrils. Then a bearded rancher spoke up.

'I reckon that critter died like he lived – trying a double-cross!'

Larry holstered his gun and went across to the fallen man. He stooped to be certain that his aim had been true – then he glanced up sharply as the rancher shouted a warning. Just in time he saw Hank, his face malevolent, level his gun. Larry's hand blurred down and up again. A split second before the vengeful gunhawk could fire, a bullet struck him clean in the forehead. He gave a shriek, clapped his hands to his face, then dropped, squirming, on to the table immediately in front of him. In a second or two his writhing ceased, and he slid to the floor – dead.

'Seems there's been a bit of cleaning up around here,' King commented. 'I reckon the air oughta smell a lot sweeter for it.'

'Get these two guys out of here,' Larry ordered briefly, glancing at the menfolk. 'I've something to say to you all afterwards.'

The assembly stirred. The two bodies were dragged away, to be buried after the minimum of legal formalities had been performed; then Larry stood on a chair and surveyed the crowded saloon.

'Listen, folks, I know I'm a stranger among you, and an

110

Englishman at that – but I think I've managed to fit in pretty well with your ways, considering how I started.'

'You sure have, feller. Don't seem like the same guy to me.'

'I'm staying on here,' Larry continued. 'I'm going to fight to the end for the inheritance I came to claim – the inheritance Makin handed over, by legal juggling, to one Simon Galt. We all know that Makin, Crawford, and Hank – who incidentally tried to burn me alive a few days ago – were all crooked. Between them they ran Buzzard's Bend pretty much as they saw fit, Crawford using his gun and hiding behind a badge – and the other his legal tricks. Hank obeyed either as it suited him. I contend that no town can thrive on those sorts of methods. A sheriff's got to be straight – right?'

'Yeah! Sure thing!'

'We'd have kicked him out before only there didn't seem t'be a way of doin' it.'

'Right now,' Larry concluded, 'there *is* no sheriff, and I'm asking you to put me in the job. I promise you that I'll clean this town of all corruption and double-dealing even if I get filled with lead doing it.'

There was a surprised silence for a moment, and Mayor Reuben was quick to speak in the midst of it.

'I don't know that we like the idea of a foreigner hustling in on us, Ashfield—'

'*Who* doesn't?' somebody demanded aggressively. 'We're not havin' any more of *your* bootlicking sheriffs, Mayor! Most folk around here know you're as big a two-timer as the guys who've been rubbed out.'

The mayor flushed angrily, but he did not pursue the subject. It was not safe. He had too few important people to support him.

111

'I reckon Larry Ashfield's the best man we could get for sheriff,' King said. 'I've seen him in action. He's got the resource, and the energy – and he isn't afraid to say what he thinks. I propose him as sheriff. Anybody second it?'

'Sure thing,' the bearded rancher said quickly, raising his hand.

'In favour?' King cried, looking about him – and without bothering to count he could see that nine-tenths of the people present raised their hands.

'No need for papers or ballots,' King said. 'OK, Larry, you're elected. Swear him in, Mayor.'

The mayor had no alternative, and went through the brief ceremony on the spot, whilst one of the men recovered the star badge from Crawford's shirt. It finished up on Larry's own breast. Then Larry called for volunteers for deputies, and several men stepped forward, including the bearded rancher. When the ceremony and appointments were over, he turned to the mayor.

'Now, Mayor, you can hand over the keys to the sheriff's office, and I'll do the rest. I'll take up my duties in the morning, but I've a special job to do first.'

Mayor Reuben looked surprised. 'Meaning?'

'I'm using my authority as sheriff to examine Cliff Makin's office. As an ordinary townsman I couldn't do it – but I can now.'

The mayor shrugged, then gave a glance about him. Several of the men within earshot began moving, and quietly left the saloon. Larry didn't notice them – but King did, and Val. They exchanged looks.

'Trouble coming,' King murmured, 'but I reckon it can't be any worse than what we've had so far.'

The mayor gave instructions for the office keys to be

taken from Crawford's distant body, lying across a table in a corner. They were handed to Larry, who pocketed them, after noticing that one of them was a master key for opening any door.

'Thanks,' Larry said briefly. 'Be seeing you again, Mayor, in the morning, when I'll take up the matter of some needed alterations in this town.'

He turned aside, joined King and Val, and together they left the saloon. On the boardwalk King gave an enquiring glance.

'You aiming to go through Makin's office right now, son?'

'Definitely – sooner the better. I'd like you to help me.'

'Sure thing,' King assented. 'But be on the look-out for trouble, Larry. Several of Makin's and Crawford's boys left the Lucky Dollar ahead of us when they heard what you were planning to do. I guess Makin's office must be loaded with incriminating evidence, and they may try to stop you.'

'Gunhawks don't worry me,' Larry said briefly. 'We're both of us armed – but I guess for safety's sake Val had better ride home again.'

'Not if I know it,' Val broke in. 'I'm only just starting to enjoy myself again. I'm not leaving.'

'OK, then let's move,' Larry said. 'The master key on this ring should fit Makin's office.'

They set off along the boardwalk. The kerosene lights were not particularly bright, so the trio could make good use of the shadows. Knowing that the gang that had worked with Crawford was still at large, they were prepared for any eventuality – but nothing happened, and they gained Makin's office safely.

After a little wrangling with the master key, Larry led

the way into the dead lawyer's office, bolting the door behind him.

The place smelled of musty deeds and stale tobacco fumes. Familiar with the layout from his previous visit, Larry went over to the safe in the corner, and struck a lucifer with which to examine it. It was by no means a modern one, but none the less impregnable for all that.

'Take dynamite to force that,' King said worriedly; then he moved swiftly and drew down the shade over the window. It would not entirely stop light, but at least it might render it less noticeable to any watchers outside.

'We can't be sure that the evidence you're wanting is in the safe,' Val said. 'Let's try everything else first; then, if all else fails, we can bring dynamite or something and blow the safe open.'

'Good idea,' Larry agreed. 'These filing cabinets are easy enough to work on. Might be something under the file of "Ashfield" – unless Crawford saw to it that it was removed.'

He took out his penknife, opened the strongest blade, and then wedged it in the topmost filing drawer. He forced back the catch, and the drawer opened. He did the same with the remaining three drawers – then, working by the light of the carefully shielded oil-lamp, they began a search.

They found stacks of correspondence and deeds of little interest. In the 'Ashfield' file there were only normal business letters referring to cattle deals and ranch matters generally, but in the invoices – a file to itself – Val came across various items connected with the Double-L that aroused her suspicions.

'These invoices show that Simon Galt is using the

Double-L as a kind of depot for cattle,' she said as the men joined her in examining the documents. 'None of the cattle has the Double-L brand, as these bills show.'

To Larry, unfamiliar with ranch routine, the bills meant little, but King snapped his forgers.

'Yeah, I get it!' he exclaimed. 'These are duplicate consignment notes of cattle sold through the Double-L, Makin having been the lawyer acting. And the cattle were probably stolen, since no Double-L brand is mentioned. Several thousand head!'

'In other words,' Val mused, 'these consignment notes point to the Double-L being used as a kind of temporary corral for rustled cattle?'

'It certainly does,' King agreed. 'I expect Crawford knew all about it, but did nothing, being on a kickback. It's up to you now, son.'

Larry gave a grim nod and put the documents in his pocket. 'First chance I get, I'll let the authorities in Prescott see these; they'll know how to act . . . but we still haven't found anything to prove that Simon Galt has no right to the Double-L.'

Larry and Val resumed searching the files, whilst King tackled the roll-top desk. Forcing open the catch, he pushed up the front and began searching through the litter of papers and drawers.

Time passed. Outside all seemed quiet, except for one occasion when it sounded as though somebody bumped against the outer office door, but a quick investigation had not revealed anybody in the darkness outside.

'Look at this!' King exclaimed suddenly, when the search was about exhausted. He had just finished rooting through the wall cupboard and had brought to light a bundle of dynamite sticks tied round with a fuse.

'Mighty convenient,' Larry said, grinning, 'but I wonder why Makin needed to keep dynamite in his office?'

'Must have been something to do with the mine, mebbe,' King replied. 'All that matters now is that we can use it on that safe! We're sure getting no results anywhere else.'

So the job of dealing with the safe began. Larry put half of the sticks inside his shirt for possible future use, then the remaining sticks were carefully arranged round the lock and packed in with heavy law-books and cushions, the fuse trailing to the far end of the office.

'We'll get outside while we blow it,' Larry murmured, lighting the fuse. 'Come on!'

The fuse spluttered, and he immediately dived for the door and wrenched it open, pushing Val out in front of him as King followed. They closed the door and then moved away to a distance. The streets appeared deserted; the Lucky Dollar had closed, and most of the townsfolk were home and asleep. The kerosene lights had been extinguished, and Buzzard's Bend had its usual after-midnight mausoleum appearance.

Then the dynamite exploded. The packing around it muffled the sound considerably, but to the three expecting it, it was shatteringly loud. They glanced about them anxiously – but nothing happened. They hurried back into the office to find part of it smoking. Furniture had been overturned, the windows had been blown out and the safe itself had its door half-off.

Quickly, Larry dragged the contents of the safe on to the floor. King and Val studied the deeds and papers as

116

they came into view – using lucifers since the oil-lamp had been buried in the debris. They gave no further thought to precautions concerning light. From the look of things no person was awake in the entire town.

But in this they were wrong. The former supporters of Makin and Crawford were anything but asleep. Since the moment the trio had left the Lucky Dollar, their movements had been constantly watched. And when watching was no longer possible the spies had listened at the door of the office. The bump one of them had given the door had nearly revealed their presence, but they had quickly withdrawn after the incident and escaped detection.

Now they were crouching outside the shattered office window, listening intently to the voices floating out to them.

'I've found something!' Val's voice was excited. 'Looks like your uncle's will, Larry!'

'This is it!' Larry exclaimed. 'We don't need any more evidence! Once the proper authorities see this, we'll soon get some action. And I'll get some myself, too. Simon Galt won't have a leg to stand on in face of this. Look – it repeats the very thing my uncle told me in his letter – that the ranch and gold mine should belong to me when he died. Here's his signature – and Cliff Makin's as the witness and lawyer.'

'What about your uncle's debts to Galt,' King asked. 'Was Makin right in paying things off the way he did?'

'Never!' Larry snapped. '*I* should have been consulted first, and anyway personal debts die with the man, unless he's the head of a company that was involved. No, the ranch and mine rightfully belong to me.'

'I was just wondering,' King said, still musing. 'It seems

strange that Makin ever kept that will by him, in face of what he did. You'd have thought he'd have destroyed it.'

'Makin was no fool,' Larry answered slowly. 'He may have kept it against the day when things got so tough he couldn't double-cross any more; then he could have 'found' the will unexpectedly, and straightened himself out by legal twisting. No smart lawyer ever destroys anything valuable. Anyway, be that as it may, I'm going to act tomorrow. Now let's get back to the spread. . . .'

Outside the office the gathered men quickly glided away, their own plans already made to deal with the situation.

7

DEATH IN THE NIGHT

Towards two in the morning a couple of horsemen rode up almost silently to the Bar-6, dismounted from their horses, and left them tied to the post of the main gate. They moved like shadows across the yard, making – as they imagined – scarcely any sound. As far as human hearing was concerned, perhaps – but other ears than human were pricked up in the gloom and nostrils were twitching curiously.

'I reckon our best chance is to break in by a side window,' one of the men murmured. 'Just as long as we don't get into one of the bedrooms.'

'The whole thing's too damned risky, if you ask me,' the other man whispered. 'We should have done as I said: attacked them on the way home, and got that will. Right now we don't even know where the durned thing is.'

'It's bound to be in their safe, and I make my living

opening safes. Quit worrying, will yuh? We couldn't attack them on the way back; they'd have heard us approaching, and we'd have risked getting lead in our bellies. You saw Ashfield's gun in action in the saloon. . . . Say, look – our luck's in. There's a window open.'

'Sure it's not a bedroom?'

'I reckon not. I figure it belongs to the living-room, going from the shape of this ranch house. Soon find out.'

On reaching the window, the taller man cautiously thrust up the sash. He muscled himself up to the sill and peered between the curtains. His guess that it was the living-foom was correct. He slid over the sill into the gloom beyond, his gun at the ready.

After a moment or two his companion slid in beside him. They could hear no sounds in the ranch house.

'This might be some kind of trap,' he breathed. 'Seems kinda queer, leavin' the window conveniently open.'

'Stop bellyaching, will yuh? Probably just for fresh air. Plenty people do it round here.'

He had guessed correctly. Larry, Val, and her father had had no thoughts of dirty work going on at their own ranch during the night.

After some awkward fumbling around, both men came upon the safe in a corner by the bureau. The taller one grinned in the gloom as he looked at it.

'Just my line,' he murmured. 'Old type with a three-figure combination. Now shut up while I listen to it play some sweet music.'

He knelt beside it, then began delicately twisting the combination knob. He heard the first click, then the second – and after a long interval the third. Gripping the bar-shaped handle, he dragged the heavy door open and peered at the vague whiteness of papers inside.

'I've gotta risk a lucifer,' he murmured, and he held it well within the safe once the flame was scratched into being. He had no need to search far: the will of Brian Ashfield was on the top of the pile, just as King had put it there before retiring.

'Found it yet?' the second man asked nervously.

'Sure thing. Let's get outa here.'

The tall one closed the door up again, twisted the knob, and then moved to the window after his companion, doubling up the will into his hip pocket. He followed his companion into the yard – then both of them froze at the sound of deep growling.

'Hell!' the smaller one gasped. 'A couple of dad-blamed Alsatians! Right in front of us. . . !'

Instantly his hand flew to his gun, but at the identical moment the Alsatians hurtled out of the dark, each one singling out a man. The two punchers went down on their backs, shouting and struggling desperately as the vicious, slavering jaws bit at them, tearing their shirts, trying to reach their throats.

The noise of the struggle and the screams of the men awakened Larry. In an instant he was out of bed, his hand grasping his gun as he hurried to the window. The starlight was just strong enough to show him what was happening. He swung round, dragged on pants and shoes then hurtled out through the living-room and on to the porch, ignoring the shouted queries of King and Val from the adjoining bedrooms.

He was down the steps and racing into the yard in a matter of seconds.

'*Come here!*' he commanded, to the snarling, biting

dogs. '*Oscar! Callie! Come here!*'

Perfectly trained, the animals obeyed. They left the two blood-streaked men on the ground and trotted over to where Larry was standing.

'*Back to bed,*' he commanded – and they departed to the shadows. Larry strode forward and tried to drag the two men to their feet. But they remained limp, completely spent. Blood was soaking their shirts from the vicious wounds in their necks. It was obvious that the dogs had attacked the vital jugulars.

'What happened?' King demanded, coming on the scene with Val behind him. They were hastily dressed in gowns, both with guns in their hands. Only moments after them came the Indian servant and his squaw.

'We've had uninvited visitors,' Larry answered grimly. 'Oscar and Callie let them through, as they're trained to do – then savaged them as they tried to leave. Better give me a hand to get them inside.'

With assistance, Larry managed to carry both men inside. Still bleeding freely, they were dumped on the hearthrug, cushions serving as pillows.

'Reckon they must have been after that will,' King said. 'Wonder if they got it?'

Whilst Larry and Val went to work as well as they could to stop the bleeding of the two barely conscious men, King went to the safe, opened it, and searched inside. He turned a grim face.

'Better search 'em. They got it.'

Larry nodded, and made a quick run through the men's pockets. He came across the will quickly enough and tossed it over to King.

'You hold it, sir; my hands are messy. Well, I'm afraid

122

we've done all we can for these men. Better send for Doc Barnes.'

Val got to her feet and hurried out to tell the Indian to ride to town for the practitioner. When she came back she saw that men were now hardly moving, their eyes closed, great wads of bandaging covering their throats and the lesser bites to their arms and bodies.

'Serves 'em right,' King said, putting the will back in the safe. 'They'll know better next time.'

'There won't be a next time,' Larry said quietly, rising. 'Both these men are dead. Shock and loss of blood, I guess.'

Val and her father exchanged looks, but said nothing.

'You two go back to bed,' Larry said. 'I'll wait up for Doc Barnes, and I'll also keep an eye on this safe. Obviously I'm not going to get much peace until the will's in the hands of the Prescott authorities – which I hope it will be by this time tomorrow.'

With a final look at the two dead men, Val and her father left the room. Larry pulled up a chair and sat down, reflecting to himself that the two gunmen had paid a mighty high price for their attempt at thieving.

At breakfast next morning he showed little signs of the night vigil he had kept.

'Doc Barnes rode out in his buckboard,' he explained, as Val and King settled at the table. 'He was able to drive the bodies back into town for the legal technicalities before burial. No blame attaches to us, of course, since they were trespassers. As sheriff I'll uphold that, too.'

'What now?' Val asked. 'Are you going straight to Prescott and get some action?'

Larry shook his head. 'Not just yet. First I'm riding out

to the Double-L with a couple of deputies and tell Simon Galt where he gets off. Once I've got rid of him I'll let the Prescott authorities have the details, and I'll take over the ranch and mine in my own name and get it legally fixed up by a good lawyer, naturally. That will bring you and me to discussing something, Val.'

She smiled but said nothing. With a murmur of apology, Larry rose from the table.

'I breakfasted earlier than you so I could get away,' he explained. 'I had Doc Barnes leave notes for my deputies to meet me here by eight-thirty. They'll be here any minute.'

'I'll come with you,' Val began, but Larry cut her short.

'Not this time, Val. This is a legal sheriff's matter, as well as my own personal business. I'll be OK with two deputies.'

He kissed her, smiled, and then, with a nod to King, took down his hat and departed. His two deputies were just in at the gate as he mounted his horse. They swung around, waited for him to catch up, then all three of them hit the trail for the Double-L.

They reached it inside an hour, and rode into the yard. Larry surveyed the prospect interestedly after he had dismounted. The spread was much bigger than the Bar-6. The ranch house was larger; the corrals more extensive.

'What now, Mr Ashfield?' one of the deputies asked, drawing his gun.

'You can put your gun back, for a start. We're here on legal business, not as a shooting party.'

Larry strode up the steps to the porch and hammered on the screen door. A half-breed, with oily black hair and wearing coat and dark trousers, presently appeared. He was a most unusual type to discover in a Western ranch.

'Yes, gentlemen?' he asked, in rather too-exact English.

'I'm Sheriff Larry Ashfield,' Larry said briefly, indicating his badge. 'I want a word with Mr Galt.'

'I'll see if he's in—'

'You can skip the formalities,' Larry broke in. 'This isn't a social call. Come on, boys.'

He jerked his head and strode through the wide hall to the doorway of the living-room. Without bothering to knock, he walked in; then slowed his pace.

The signs of his late uncle's wealth were everywhere – in the furniture, the polished brassware, the gleaming glass fronts of large bookcases. Here was a luxury ranch, and in such a remote spot it could only have been furnished at enormous expense. Even the log walls were treated with some kind of composition to make them appear snowy white, deepening to mauve where they joined the ceiling.

Larry's main interest, however, was concentrated on the man seated eating breakfast by the sunny window. The table was small, perfectly laid, and the breakfast appetizing. Even the coffee jug was solid silver. The man who sat amidst these evidences of wealth was unusually fat, with a round, disarmingly bland face and pink cheeks. He looked curiously like a newly washed baby. His hair was grey, and he ate daintily. He was wearing an elaborate satin dressing-gown.

'Good morning, gentlemen,' he greeted, as the three men came towards him. 'I gather you are in a hurry since my servant did not announce you.'

'I take it you are Simon Galt?'

'Yes, indeed.' Simon Galt breathed heavily and got to his feet. 'You, of course, are Larry Ashfield, our newly elected sheriff. Congratulations.'

He held out a plump hand, but Larry ignored it.

'You can skip the cordiality, Mr Galt,' he said bluntly. 'We are not exactly friends.'

'No? What a pity. I like everybody to be friends with me.' Galt smiled, and it increased the width of his three chins; but the prominent eyes had no humour in them. They were stone-grey, and staring fixedly.

'All right, Galt, suppose we get down to business,' Larry suggested. 'I'm here to claim this ranch, and the mine. Since you already know I'm sheriff, I assume you also know that I am Brian Ashield's nephew.'

'I gathered as much. Oh, come now, gentlemen, you have had a hard ride in crisp morning air – how about some coffee? Or some grilled ham and eggs. Or—'

'We've had breakfast,' Larry interrupted. He took the will from his pocket and held it out – from a safe distance.

'Here is my uncle's will, Galt. It proves that he bequeathed this ranch and the nearby mine to me.'

'I'll take your word for it,' Galt sat down again. 'You will forgive me, gentlemen, if I proceed with my breakfast? I much prefer my ham and eggs to be hot.'

Deliberately, he resumed eating. Larry exchanged glances with his deputies. They had expected Galt to be perhaps a trifle unusual, but they had never bargained for this. He spoke perfectly; his manners were beyond reproach. There was not one trace of Western ruggedness about him.

'So your uncle bequeathed the mine to you as well?' he asked, sitting back and munching complacently. 'Oh, do sit down, gentlemen. You worry me standing up.'

'We'll go right on worrying you,' Larry said, putting the will back in his pocket. 'I'm giving you twelve hours to quit

126

this ranch, Galt. Be out of here by sunset tonight, with your personal belongings, and nothing more. If you touch one thing that belongs to me – which formerly belonged to my uncle – I'll get it back the tough way. Even as it is, I intend to start proceedings against you for taking this ranch over. The Prescott authorities will deal with that.'

'Quite an enterprising young man, are you not?' Galt asked.

'I know my rights. You got this place through some double-crossing work on Makin's part – and I know *why* you got it. So you could make it a depot for stolen cattle, amongst other things.'

'Other things?'

'I'm talking about the gold mine. Every penny you have made out of that since the day my uncle died will have to be repaid – to me. I'll take court action over it.'

Galt smiled, and buttered a piece of toast. Larry scowled and turned away. 'Don't forget: sunset tonight.'

He strode towards the doorway, his two deputies behind him. Then Galt's voice stopped him.

'Mr Ashfield, I think you are forgetting something.'

'For instance?' Larry demanded.

'An order to quit.' Galt gave a dry chuckle. 'You have shown me a will, purporting to be that of your uncle – but you have neglected the formality of *legally* ordering me out. Naturally I do not intend to budge just because you tell me to.'

Larry glanced at his deputies, who were looking sheepish.

'Still quite young in the business of sheriff, perhaps?' Galt enquired, raising his coffee cup.

Larry returned to the table. 'I'll be back with that quit

notice soon enough. You just make preparations for getting out, that's all.'

Galt simply gazed with his cold, fishlike eyes.

'I think it only fair to remind you, Mr Ashfield, that, to be legal, the quit notice must be signed by the mayor. Somehow, I do not think he will oblige you, being a very good friend of mine.'

'He'll do as he's told, even if I have to hold a gun at his head.'

'In that case he can claim he had to sign under duress. A court of law, which you seem so anxious to involve in the proceedings, would not look favourably on that move.'

Larry latched his thumbs on his gun belts and contemplated the obese Galt thoughtfully.

'Obviously,' he said. 'You are not the rightful owner, otherwise you wouldn't go through such contortions to try and stop me throwing you out.'

'I think,' Galt said, rising to his feet again, 'that you will have far more peace of mind, Mr Ashfield, if you forgot your inheritance entirely. The present legal situation is that it is mine, and I intend to remain here. I don't think all the authorities in the world will be able to help you. If by some miracle you do get the mayor to sign the quit notice without intimidating him, all the better for you. Then I will go – and fight you by law to recover what has legally been made mine.'

'This will proves it isn't legally yours,' Larry retorted. 'So you'd better start packing. I'll be back later.'

Larry turned away angrily and left the living-room. Galt watched him go, through the window, then he clapped his hands sharply. The half-breed came in at a run.

'Get Mr Denton here at once,' he ordered, and with a

nod the servant hurried off.

Denton, when he arrived, was a big, square-shouldered man with a beef-red face and swaggering walk. He eyed Galt in surprise as he came into the living-room.

'Something wrong, boss? I'm pretty busy at the mine—'

'You may have nothing to be busy about if we don't get some kind of action,' Galt told him, turning from the window. 'I've just had a visit from our dashing young sheriff – Larry Ashfield.'

'Nephew of the old boy who had this place?'

'The same.' Galt sat down, breathing heavily, motioning Denton to pull up a chair.

'Nothing he can do, is there?' Denton demanded.

'On the contrary, there's the devil of a lot he can do – and he isn't a man who scares easily. He has a will of his uncle's, which he can only have obtained from Makin's office. If that damned idiot had taken my advice in the first place and destroyed that will this wouldn't have happened.'

'Why didn't he?' Denton asked, puzzled.

'Because he wanted to keep a hold over me. If I stepped out of line with him he could have pitched me out by "finding" that will and letting Larry Ashfield take over – legally. Makin would have lost plenty in the doing, of course, but he would have preferred that to having me putting a spoke in his wheel.'

'You mean this Ashfield can throw you out?'

'He has already tried it. I was able to refuse, there being no order to quit as yet. I think Ashfield may manage to get that somehow. If he does, I've no alternative but to go. I have a plan to stop that, which I'll explain in a moment or two. Right now, my reason for sending for you is to tell you to keep the mine, no matter what happens. If Ashfield should get the ranch he'll automatically try and take over the mine. Stop him at all costs. We're doing too well out of it to lose it.'

Denton looked troubled. 'I can mebbe hold on to the mine against all the men Ashfield can dig up – but I can't fight the federal authorities if they step in – as they look likely for doing.'

Galt pondered as he lighted a cigar. 'Maybe you won't have to fight anybody,' he said. 'Which brings me to my scheme. Now, listen carefully. . . .'

And whilst Denton did as he was told, Larry and his deputies rode back into Buzzard's Bend.

'You mean to try and make the mayor sign that quit order?' one of the deputies asked, as the main street was reached.

'Yes. He can bring all the charges of intimidation he wants if it ever gets into court to be argued. At the moment my main concern is getting his signature. It would have helped if you two had told me we needed such an order.'

The second deputy shrugged. 'We're new to the job, same as you are.' Then he brightened at a thought. 'But mebbe you'll be able to find plenty of quit order blanks in Crawford's office.'

He was right. Larry filled out the details on one of them, and then, still with his deputies, made his way to Mayor Reuben's office. He was within, making a pretence of working, but it was plain he had seen the three approach. The net-covered window was directly in front of his desk.

'Well, Sheriff?' he asked, endeavouring to sound formal

and cordial – and not doing either properly.

'Get your signature on that, Mayor.' Larry tossed down the form on the desk.

There was silence as the mayor read the form through; then he shook his head.

'I'm not doing it, Ashfield. I'm not that crazy – but you must be. Trying to order out Simon Galt without a ghost of a legal reason for doing so.'

Larry held out the will signed by his uncle.

'There's my reason,' he said coldly. 'Now get that form signed.'

'But – but Galt is my best friend.'

'Be damned to that! This is business. Blast you, man, hurry up! The whole thing's legal, and it's got to be done. Get busy.'

Still the mayor hesitated. 'If I sign this, Galt will probably kill me.'

'Stop clowning around, Mayor,' one of the deputies said roughly. 'Get the dad-blamed thing signed. Unless you want persuading into it. I wouldn't be beyond giving you a work-over, Reuben! You're as big a twister as the rest of them in this infernal—'

The deputy broke off, flinging himself down as there was a sudden vicious splintering of the window glass before the desk. Larry flung himself backwards, and the third man dodged behind the desk. Mayor Reuben, however, had fallen back in his chair, his head lolling, crimson from bullet wounds staining the front of his shirt.

Larry jumped up and dived for the door. He was just in time to see three horsemen speeding out of the main street's far end, watched by the surprised people on the

131

boardwalks and in the street. Not that gunplay was foreign to Buzzard's Bend, only it was rarely done so ruthlessly.

Larry hesitated for a moment over pursuing the horsemen and then thought better of it. Their start was too great. He came back into the office to find his two deputies grim-faced.

'I guess you'll get no quit order signed by this guy,' one of them said. 'Or anything else. Whoever it was got him.'

'Men employed by Galt obviously,' Larry muttered. 'OK, that washes up the quit order and leaves Galt legally sitting pretty for the moment. I certainly can't prove he did this, though I can think a good deal. My only move now is to ride out to Prescott – and that's what I'm going to do.'

'Need us?' the second deputy asked.

'No, thanks. I'll ride alone: but you two can keep the town in order while I'm gone. I'll call in at the spread for food and provisions, and then be on my way. Seems only a marshal can settle this.'

He hurried out of the office and leapt to the saddle of his horse at the tie rack. Loosening the reins, he swung the animal's head round and rode at top speed out of the main street, never slackening the pace until he had reached the Bar-6; then, as he entered the main yard, he looked about him in surprise. Several of the men from the outfit were hastily bandaged and had deserted their usual work in the corrals.

'What goes on?' Larry demanded, as the foreman, his forehead bound up, came hurrying across to him.

'We've been attacked, Mr Ashfield,' the man answered, his leathery face grim. 'A score of gunmen came ridin' down upon us not ten minutes ago. We were caught by surprise and put up the best fight we could. But they got Miss King!'

'*Got her?*' Larry dropped from the saddle. 'You don't mean she's—'

'They rode away with her. Got her all bound up so's she couldn't escape. Mr King got shot, an' we got him to bed. . . .'

Larry did not wait for any more. He twirled round and dashed for the porch steps. In a matter of seconds he was through the living-room and in King's bedroom. King was lying flat, a bandage about his head, and another on his muscular arm.

'Glad you got back, son,' he muttered, evidently still fully conscious. 'Sure was some dust-up not so long ago – mebbe Galt's men.'

'No doubt of it,' Larry retorted. 'I'm going right after Val this moment. How are you fixed? Is it bad?'

'I guess not. Flesh wound across the scalp and a chunk torn outa my arm. It left me sick for a while, and the boys put me in bed here. They put up the best fight they could. Look after yourself, Larry.'

'I'm more concerned about Val,' he answered, and hurried out again.

Half-way across the living room he slowed down and looked at the table. He had just noticed a letter lying on it, the envelope addressed to him. He snatched it up and looked at the neat handwriting. Immediately he assumed it was Galt's.

He was right. The letter was brief, but very much to the point.

Dear Mr Ashfield,
I would be glad if you would ride over to the Double-L, and bring with you your uncle's will. I am sure we can

133

straighten matters out satisfactorily, concerning Miss King,
I mean.

   Simon Galt.

'Not so smart as he thinks,' Larry muttered. 'This letter is black-and-white proof that there is a will.'

He put it in his pocket – where the will still lay folded – and then hurried outside. He only paused long enough to tell the foreman to fetch Dr Barnes to attend to the injured; then he swung to the saddle and rode hell for leather down the trail to the Double-L. Within forty-five minutes he was in Simon Galt's living-room.

'I thought you wouldn't waste any time, Ashfield,' Galt said drily, drawing at his cigar. 'Have a seat.'

'Never mind that. Where's Miss King?'

'Nearby, and quite comfortable – at the moment. I understand that my boys played rather rough down at the Bar-6. Believe me, that was none of my doing. I simply told them to fetch Miss King here, no matter what the consequences. Apparently, they interpreted my orders a trifle too literally.'

'I suppose you didn't tell anybody to shoot the mayor, either?'

Galt smiled broadly and his chins expanded. 'Matter of fact, I did. I can admit it openly since we have no witnesses in this room. I thought the mayor might weaken and sign that quit notice so I made sure.'

Galt moved to a chair and sprawled in it. He dusted tobacco ash from the lapel of his gown.

'Mr Ashfield, I am going to make you a proposition. I don't want Miss King. I merely brought her here so she can become a lever for our little deal. I am prepared to

134

hand her back to you, in perfect health, in return for your uncle's will.'

'You're admitting, then, that this will has some danger value?'

'Yes, I admit it. Forgive my earlier strategy, Mr Ashfield. Things worked out just as I had hoped. You went to the mayor's office, and in that time I managed to remove Miss King, or, rather, my boys did. I took the risk that when the mayor was shot you would be shot too. Had that happened I would have returned Miss King to the Bar-6, found a way to get the will from your dead body, and so make myself safe. However, none of that came to pass. You are here – with the will, I assume?'

'I have it, and I'm sticking to it. . . .' Larry suddenly dropped his hand to his right gun, but Galt had anticipated the action and an automatic flashed up from his gown pocket and remained steady.

'I shouldn't be too impetuous, Mr Ashfield,' he murmured. 'So you intend to retain the will? You do not value Miss King's life any more highly than that?'

Larry gave a quick look about him. Galt chuckled.

'Don't waste your time looking for ways of escape. There is none. And now I intend to progress. Maybe you would like to see Miss King?'

Larry did not answer; so Galt got to his feet and motioned to the hall. He never relaxed his vigilance as he walked to a door and pushed it open, motioning Larry into the room beyond. It was a bedroom, neatly furnished. On the bed, her hands bound to the head of the bed and her ankles to the foot, lay Val. She turned her head as the two men came in.

'Larry!' she cried, struggling to free herself. 'What –

what happened to Dad?'

'He's alive. Just flesh wounds. I—'

'Stand still, Ashfield,' Gait ordered. 'One step nearer to Miss King and I'll let you have it. . . . As I told you,' he continued, 'Miss King is quite comfortable. I will release her and return her to you if you will give me the will.'

'I don't get it,' Larry said bluntly. 'You've got the gun. What's stopping you taking the will from me?'

'Nothing – but there is more to it than that. You will also write a letter abandoning all claim in the Double-L and the mine attached to it. I want you to do everything of your own – er – free will. Understand?'

'Supposing I tell you to smash your head against a wall?'

'I am afraid I would have to decline,' Galt answered. 'However, if you don't do as I ask, let me show you what will happen.'

He moved backwards, keeping his automatic at the ready. From a corner he dragged forth a large box, its top riddled with air holes. The further side of the box had a glass window inset, and through it Larry could dimly see something moving. When the box was brought nearer, so that it stood beside the bed, he could see the object clearly.

'*A rattlesnake*!' he exclaimed.

'Precisely,' Galt agreed. 'You will notice that the catch to the lid of this box has a string attached, so it can be pulled from a distance. The rattler has not had its fangs drawn. . . . Miss King's death from a rattler bite could never be called murder. Rattlers abound in this part of the world.'

Galt paused and added coldly, 'The decision is in your hands, Mr Ashfield.'

Larry looked at the girl's drawn, anxious face, then at the deadly rattler.

'You win,' he said. 'Release her.'

'Not yet, my friends. You will be kind enough to write the letter I shall dictate first. Come with me.'

Larry went out of the room with Galt behind him. Val watched the door close and pulled hard on her bound wrists and ankles, but she could not budge them. She relaxed, breathing hard, cramped from strain. Her eyes travelled to the box at the bedside. The glass front was turned away from her but she could hear the slithering of the deadly reptile as it moved in its prison.

It was the sudden thump of the lid rising and falling that made her look again at the box. She frowned; then her heart began to hammer violently as she saw the wicked head of the snake just emerging from under the lid. How it had come loose she did not know, unless in demonstrating the catch Galt had not closed it properly.

'*Larry*!' Val screamed, lashing her body helplessly to try and get free. '*Larry! The, snake*—!'

Nobody came in response to her shouts, probably because her voice did not travel through the closed door, across the wide hall, and through another closed door. Besides, the more she cried, the more the rattler was attracted to her. It slid gently out of the box and lay for a moment on the floor, like a shining length of multi-coloured rope.

Val lay rigid, staring at it, her fingers clenched above the ropes holding her wrists. Presently its head reared. Val shouted again, remembering that as long as the reptile was startled it would not strike. Its tail began to rattle in impatience, and as long as that continued she was safe.

'*Larry*!' she yelled frantically. '*Larry*!'

The rattling stopped. The vile head was swinging in the air, the merciless eyes fixed upon her. She felt perspiration wet on her face, trickling down on to the pillow. Hypnotically, the snake's eyes held hers. It was all set for attack, its rattling tail still. Then the door clicked open and it fell back on its coils, rattling fiercely, again disturbed.

'My God!' Larry gasped – and ignoring Galt, the gun, and the danger, he dived forward.

With a lightning movement, he seized the reptile by the centre of its body and flung it violently into the box, slamming the lid down on it. Galt said nothing for a moment as Larry fiddled with the box catch.

'This is loose,' Larry said bitterly. 'Better get it fixed if you want to keep your filthy playmate.'

'I'm sorry you were so inconvenienced, Miss King,' Galt murmured. 'An accident, believe me.'

Val couldn't speak. She was breathing hard, her face white and glistening. Larry took out his penknife and slashed through the ropes holding her. She stirred slowly and rubbed her cramped limbs.

'You are at liberty to leave whenever you wish,' Galt said. 'Mr Ashfield and I have come to quite a satisfactory understanding.'

'From your point of view only,' Larry retorted.

He lifted Val from the bed and set her on her feet. She began to move shakily, his arm about her waist. Galt held the door open for them, smiling only with his lips.

Without a word Larry led the girl through the hall and to the porch. Once in the fresh air she began to recover.

'Let's go,' Larry said, nodding towards his horse, and

Val preceded him down the steps. He raised her to the saddle, swung up behind her, and then rode the animal quickly away to the trail.

'Does this mean that Galt's gotten all he wanted?' Val asked at last, when the journey was half over.

'For the moment,' Larry acknowledged. 'It was that, or the end of you. Only one answer, I guess. . . . But it isn't the finish. Not by a long way.'

8

SNAKE
VENGEANCE

Once Larry and Val returned to the Bar-6 they had their
hands full keeping things in order, several of the men in
the outfit being too hurt to work, and King himself resting
up until he had recovered from his flesh wounds. Dr
Barnes called for the second time during the afternoon,
dourly remarked that all the victims were progressing satisfactorily, and that he ought to move in permanently as a
resident physician; then he departed with the assurance
that he would look in again the following day.

It was therefore around eight before Larry and Val had
a settled opportunity to discuss matters over supper.

'I can't help but feel that it's my fault that you've lost
everything you've been fighting for, Larry.'

'That's ridiculous.' He patted her hand as it lay on the
table. 'You are the most valuable possession I have – and
Galt was smart enough to realize it. I wrote a letter under his

dictates, by which I gave up all claims in the Double-L and the gold mine, and I handed him the will – but I also took good care to notice where the safe was at the same time.'

'You mean you're going to risk trying to get the letter and will back?' Val shook her head. 'That's just what Galt will be expecting, and the spread will be bristling with guns. And even if you could get to the safe, how will you open it? If it comes to that, where's the guarantee it will contain what you're looking for?'

'It will: I'm sure of it. Galt wouldn't trust his most important papers to anything less than a safe. As for opening the safe, that won't be difficult. I kept back half of the sticks of that dynamite we found in Makin's office – they're still in my saddle-bag, They made short work of Makin's safe, and will do the same for Galt's.'

'But how are you going to actually get into his living-room? His ranch is crawling with men. . . .'

'I've got it all mapped out, Val, and it's going to be a one-man job. I must handle it in my own way. I propose to set fire to several of the outhouses and start plenty of activity in that direction. Galt will be bound to join the fire-fighters, and when that happens I'll get busy and recover those documents.'

'I hope you're right,' Val said uneasily. 'He strikes me as being much more dangerous than anybody we've yet come up against.'

Larry only smiled and went on with his meal. When the meal was over he made the final preparations for his one-man raid on the Double-L. He removed the spare dyna-mite from his saddlebag and packed it in a satchel, which could be easily carried on his shoulder. He also packed some thin rope.

When real darkness came he set off, his guns loaded and his belts full of cartridges, the satchel tied to the horn of his saddle. Those men who were fit were left in the Bar-6 outfit, ordered to remain on guard in case anything was attempted on Val and her father, though this seemed unlikely now that Galt had got what he wanted.

The Double-L was in darkness when Larry approached it. He dismounted perhaps half a mile from it, standing for a long time with his horse in the deep shadow of a cedar tree. Carefully he surveyed the ranch, looking for any men who were possibly hidden about it.

Securing his horse's reins, he took down the satchel on to his shoulder, lifted his right-hand gun and then made a swift, crouching circuit of the ranch so that he eventually came to its rear. From this point he began to advance, the only sound he made coming from the dry grass beneath him. After a while a dog barked somewhere on the spread, a deep and powerful baying that reminded him of the Alsatians guarding the Bar-6. But he was confident he could handle the animal if he had to.

At length he gained the first outhouses and felt in his pocket for lucifers. Just as he was doing so, a shadowy figure came into view carrying a rifle – obviously one of the Double-L outfit on patrol. Larry did not wait to have the rifle levelled at him. He lashed out the butt of his heavy gun and struck the man behind the ear before he had fully grasped what was happening. With a grunt he buckled to the ground, his rifle clattering from him. The noise of it set the dog barking again, this time from a much nearer point, and apparently coming nearer still.

Larry looked about him quickly, struck his lucifer, and put the flame under the piles of straw just inside the

142

outhouse's open doorway. Then, as the fire instantly kindled, he swung round to see the green eyes of a dog bobbing towards him as the animal hurtled forward.

The dog leapt straight at him – a mastiff, and what it lacked in training it made up for in ferocity. Larry found himself stumbling backwards, the heavy, snarling head only a few inches from his face. He flung up his left hand and closed it round the dog's bottom jaw, holding it in a steel grip so that it could not bite. Then, still clinging on by sheer muscular effort, he twisted the gun in his right hand and slammed it down again and again on the back of the brute's head. It growled and groaned by turns, writhing at each blow and striving to close its jaws. Larry struck yet again, and this time he stunned the creature into unconsciousness. It relaxed across him. He dragged out his saliva-fouled hand from the sharp teeth and staggered to his feet.

There were sounds of hurrying footsteps. He bounded away from the blaze into the darker shadows at the opposite side of the yard and watched intently what happened.

The men of the outfit, attracted by the barking of the dog, and evidently seeing the fire, came on the scene in another moment or two. They rushed in and out of the smoke for a while, then orders were shouted, and the men began the job of transporting water and fire-fighting equipment. Larry grinned as he watched them, then, as the fire got a stronger hold and consequently increased its glare, he escaped round the back of the ranch and, by degrees, worked his way to the side of it where the living-room lay.

He made no immediate moves. He stopped where he could watch the porch, and it was not long before he saw

Galt himself appear, hastily dressed in shirt and riding-pants, his gross figure outlined against the blaze, followed by his half-breed servant. He shouted instructions to his servant who ran on to join the fire-fighters. Had Galt then gone with him, Larry would have carried out his plan of breaking into the living-room through the window and doing his utmost to ransack the safe before Galt came back. But instead Galt stopped and looked about him, which – from Larry's point of view – made things all the easier.

He quickly vaulted the rail round the porch and sped across to where Galt stood. Galt swung round at the sounds of Larry's approach and snatched at his gun – then he gasped and reeled as iron knuckles slammed under his jaw. Unable to keep his balance, he rolled into the hall through the front doorway. Instantly Larry was after him, stopping only to bolt the front door behind him. The hall was dark, but the flames from across the yard cast a faint reflection through the hall window.

'Get up!' Larry commanded, prodding Galt's dim figure with his gun. 'And I'll take that. . . .'

He took Galt's .45 from him and put it into his belt, then he sent the fat rancher stumbling forward into the living-room. Again Larry secured the door, then he looked at Galt steadily. Everything in the room was brightly visible without the need of the oil-lamp, thanks to the flames from the raging outhouse.

'Maybe I should have expected this, Ashfield,' Galt said, fingering his bruised chins.

'I'm surprised you didn't,' Larry retorted. 'Or maybe you thought your patrols and mastiff were sufficient? I can think up strategy the same as you can. Now sit down by the safe over there.'

Having no alternative, Galt obeyed, keeping his hands up. Once he had got him into the chair Larry lowered his satchel from his shoulder and used some of the thin rope within it to bind Galt hand and foot.

'I brought this to deal with your servant,' Larry said, 'but it'll do nicely for you.' When the man was secured Larry holstered his gun.

'If anybody comes chasing you, Galt – as they probably will if the blaze doesn't die down – you'll not answer,' he said. 'In fact, I'll make sure of it.'

Next he used his own kerchief to make a gag, leaving Galt glaring at him fixedly.

'According to my calculations,' Larry continued, reaching again into his satchel, 'the fire will spread to destroy every outhouse – and that gives me plenty time. The wind's the wrong way for the sparks to be carried to this ranch house, not because I'd have any objections to burning you out but because I've no wish to damage my own property – not to mention my will!'

Galt shifted and stirred. He could not budge the thin but strong rope with which he was fastened, so he sat and watched to see what Larry would do next. His eyes glinted in fear as Larry removed a stick of dynamite.

'I was going to use this to blow your safe, but now I've found a better use for it.' Larry's voice was cold and deadly.

He tied the stick to a leg of the chair, right next to Galt's own trussed left leg, and attached a fuse to it. He brought out a lucifer and waved it in front of Galt's bulging eyes.

'You've got a simple choice. Either you open the safe for me, nice and easy, or I'll blow your leg off! If you agree to open the safe, just nod your head. Doesn't matter to me

145

which you choose. I've other sticks I can use to blow the safe afterwards!'

He struck the lucifer, and bent towards the fuse.

Frantic, Galt nodded his head vigorously. Larry smiled grimly, blowing out the lucifer as he straightened.

'I'm freeing your right hand, Galt, so you can work the combination.' He seized the back of the chair and heaved it forward, so that Galt was seated directly in front of the safe.

With trembling fingers, Galt worked the combinations. The safe door swung open.

Quickly, Larry retied Galt's arm and heaved the chair clear. Then he struck another lucifer and peered inside the safe.

He knew he was on the right track by the savage movements Galt kept making to free himself, and sure enough, under a pile of deeds which had probably been put in last, Larry came to his own letter and the will, both fastened together by a rubber band.

'Just what I wanted,' he said drily. 'I know I've no mayor to sign the quit order, but I'll have one by tomorrow, I'll make sure he isn't crooked like the last one. You're all washed up, Galt!'

'Who sez so?' snapped a voice from the shadows.

Larry turned his head, dropping his hand to his gun, then froze as a bullet struck the safe behind him.

'Better not, Ashfield! Git your hands up!'

Larry obeyed, the will and letter still in his left hand. The shadowy figure came across and took them from him, his remaining hand holding the gun. 'Good job I looked in, Mr Galt,' the man said, turning slightly. 'I found the ranch door bolted on the inside, so looked through the

146

window and saw this goin' on. Simple enough to get in here with the window being a bit open. I waited until this guy was sticking his head inside the safe and he never saw or heard a thing.'

The man put the letter and will in his shirt pocket and then used the hand to pull down the gag from Galt's mouth. He produced a penknife and cut through the ropes binding his wrists and ankles to the chair. Larry, on his feet, stood watching narrowly in the fire-painted gloom.

'Good work, Swainson,' Galt said, gasping slightly for breath, and struggling to his feet. 'Swainson is my fore-man,' he added, turning to Larry. 'A smart man.'

The foreman smiled and handed Galt the will and letter before taking his gun from Larry's belt and handing it across also. Larry's own guns he took away and tossed into another chair across the room.

'How's the fire?' Galt asked briefly.

'Bein' brought under control, I guess. I came for you to report, and also to find out why you hadn't come out t'see what was goin' on.'

'Get back on the job,' Galt instructed. 'I'll take care of Ashfield personally.'

The foreman nodded, crossed to the door and unbolted it. After he had left, Galt moved towards the oil-lamp, his gun still trained on Larry. One-handedly, he lighted it from the lucifers kept beside it.

'Now, Ashfield, we're back where we started.' Galt pulled up the chair, easing his gross bulk into it. Evidently he was still feeling some discomfort from Larry's earlier treatment of him.

His gun was pointed unwaveringly at Larry's chest.

'You leave me in the interesting position of deciding how to dispose of you. You've only yourself to blame. Had you not came back, I might have left you to your own devices. As it is, I have to decide whether to simply put a bullet through you – or,' his voice rose venomously, 'strap that dynamite to you, as you threatened to do to me! I rather like that idea! Let me think about it. . . . Take off that satchel with the dynamite, and lay it down – slowly! Try throwing it and I'll shoot you dead now!'

Larry obeyed, easing the strap from his shoulder, and letting the satchel slip to the floor. Galt watched his actions intently.

'You are a trespasser, who has also committed arson. I have all the men in my outfit as witnesses, so no court can accuse me of murder.' Galt's bulging eyes glinted with anticipation.

Larry was facing death and he knew it. All he could do now was to try and stall.

'Before I die, Galt, how about satisfying my curiosity on a few points? How exactly did you tie in with Makin?'

Galt gave a fleshy chuckle. 'Playing for time, eh? Don't want to die just yet? Very well – I rather like the idea of you knowing everything before you die. . . .' he shrugged, shifting his bulk in the chair. The gun never wavered.

'You can have the facts, since they won't do you any good now. When your uncle died, Cliff Makin was his lawyer. Your uncle had such absolute faith in Makin – so he told me – that he fell into the habit of not even reading the many legal documents he had to sign from time to time. That was when Makin fixed it so your uncle unwittingly signed a document which contained a clause saying that, at his death, the disposal of his property and effects was at the discretion of Makin.'

'Which the will offset?' Larry asked.

'Correct. Makin thought he was all set when your uncle died unexpectedly in an accident. I'd been in contact with Makin for some time – I was living m Montana then, as manager of a big trading concern – and was disposing of cattle amongst other things, which he had obtained from various parts of the country. Makin, in fact, was the brains behind an enormous rustling concern, operating so efficiently, and over such a wide area, that no authorities could pin him down. This ranch seemed to him a good spot to which many cattle could be brought. It's large, well hidden, and central for all neighbouring territory. He couldn't handle a repository for himself, having his lawyer's business to watch, so he called me in. I took over, as an apparent new owner. The story Makin told was that I had loaned your uncle money and was taking it back in this fashion.'

'And the gold mine?' Larry asked grimly.

'As to that, Makin increased the number of men working on it, dismissing all those who had worked for your uncle. Nothing crooked in the working of it. The gold is mined, sent to a bank in San Francisco under guard, and there changed into cash. It is in my name, since I am supposed to be the owner of this ranch.'

'And you, Makin, and the mayor – and maybe one or two others, cashed in on the gold returns?'

'It used to work that way,' Gait smiled.

'How do you mean?'

'I mean that whilst Makin was alive he could only get any money from gold returns by my signing the cheque. If I didn't sign it he could – by finding the will of your uncle

– throw me out of here. Thereby I would lose the mine, the ranch, and all the lot. His idea in making me the signatory for the cheques was to keep his own name out of it, even if it did put him partly in my hands. Still, with the hold he had over me, it was as broad as long. The mayor came in for cuts from time to time. When Makin was killed the picture changed. It left me as the owner of the mine, with no need to share the proceeds with anybody.'

'Had I not stepped in and spoiled it for you,' Larry said.

'Yes, indeed,' Galt smiled. 'But now that problem is about to be eliminated—'

Galt's smile vanished abruptly as, with sudden, terrific force, Larry lashed up his right foot so it struck underneath the satchel at his feet. Not being very heavy, it flew upwards straight into Galt's face. A split second later he flung himself with all his weight and power into Galt where he sat in the chair. Galt and the chair toppled over backwards before he had the chance to fire his gun.

Galt's head seemed to explode with the blow he received across the bridge of his nose. Larry dived his hand into Galt's shirt pocket, endeavouring to drag out the will and letter – but the pocket was on the small side and his hand jammed. That gave Galt his chance. He hammered his fists into Larry's face, pounding it ruthlessly; then he brought up his knees. Unable to help himself Larry rolled sideways. Just in time he blocked Galt's arm as, his gun in his hand, he slammed it down fiercely.

For a second or so it was a battle of sheer muscular strength between them, and Larry won it. Panting, he twisted Galt's wrist until the gun dropped. Then he sprang to his feet, dragging Galt's gross bulk up after him. A blow in the eyes sent Galt staggering towards the huge book-case. He struck it, shattering the glass. Dazed, he swung away from it and fell into the nearby chair.

Instantly he was up again, a gun in his hand. Larry realized sickly that it was one of his own two guns that the foreman had flung there earlier.

'All right, you're dying right now!' Galt snapped; then for some obscure reason he broke off with an anguished scream, the gun dropping from his fingers. He reeled, clutching at his wrist. Larry stared in amazement, then his gaze dropped to a multicoloured coil sinking back on itself on the floor, its tail rattling in startled irritation.

'*The snake!*' Galt shouted hoarsely. '*It got me. . . .*'

Larry snatched the gun from the floor where Galt had dropped it and fired at the reptile savagely, three times, before he got a direct hit. He looked away from the quivering, half-severed coils to where Galt was lurching by the fireplace, all the fight blasted out of him.

'You should have had the catch fixed on that box of yours,' Larry said grimly, taking the letter and will from Galt's shirt pocket. 'I'm not wasting any sympathy on you, Galt, after the way you treated Val this morning. And I don't know anything about snakebites anyway.'

'*The fire!*' Galt panted hoarsely, his face gleaming with sweat. 'That's what did it – it was scared of the fire. Got out through the bedroom window maybe – or by the door. I – I can *feel* the damned poison in my arm. Get – get my servant for me. . . .'

He reeled backwards and slumped into the chair, holding his arm and whimpering like a gross baby. Ignoring him, Larry picked up his second gun and, without a word, turned to the window. He scrambled through it, dropped into the yard and looked about him. The fire was well under control, the flames diminishing – but the smoke was densely thick. Using it as cover, he made his way quickly across the yard, then suddenly he ran into a hurrying cowpuncher. He seized the surprised man by the scruff of the neck.

'Listen you,' Larry shook him fiercely, 'your boss has been bitten by his pet rattler. I'm his enemy, but I don't leave a man to just die, no matter how much I hate him. Get him a doctor, quick. Now blow.'

Larry yanked out his gun and waited until the startled man had vanished in the smoke. Then, feeling his conscience was eased on this point, Larry hurried on his way to find his horse, and succeeded in getting clear without further hindrance.

He was not pursued. Possibly the need to watch the fire, and the condition of Galt, demanded the men's attention at the ranch. Whatever the cause Larry rode back through the night without the thunder of hoofs behind him, and he arrived back in the Bar-6.

As he dismounted outside the ranch house he noticed that the lights were still on. Suddenly the door opened and Val King ran out to greet him.

'Larry!' she cried in joy. 'You made it! We've been waiting up for you . . . I heard you riding up—'

Then the girl was in his arms, and neither spoke for a moment. Then together, they mounted the steps and went in through the open door, Larry's arm about the girl's waist.

'Did you say "we" just now, Val?' Larry asked, puzzled, as the girl disengaged his arm gently and went ahead of him into the living-room.

To his astonishment there were two men seated at the table, drinking coffee. One was the girl's father. He looked much better, despite the considerable bandaging about him. He waved cheerfully, smiling, but did not get up. To Larry's further amazement, the second seated figure was Judge Gascoigne. He stood up, adjusting his steel-rimmed spectacles, his round face smiling pleasantly.

'Hello, son! Haven't seen you since the courtroom – but I've been hearing a mighty lot about you. How'd you make out with Galt?'

'I got what I went for – but I had a rough time.' Larry came over to the table, putting the will and letter upon it. Before he said anything further, he set fire to the letter over the oil-lamp and threw the last charred fragments into the empty fire grate.

'Here's some coffee,' Val said, handing it across. 'Now, what happened?'

'Before I go into that, perhaps someone could tell me how come Judge Gascoigne is here?'

'That was Val's idea,' King said, giving his daughter a proud glance. 'After you left earlier tonight, she took the buckboard into town to the judge's house. My foreman went with her for protection—'

'Not that we needed it,' the girl put in, taking up the story. 'We drove to the judge's house, and. . . .' she hesitated, looking at the judge with a slightly embarrassed smile.

'She woke me up – and at the most ungodly hour!' Gascoigne said. 'Naturally, I'd heard all about your election, and what had happened in the saloon. Not to mention the shooting of Mayor Reuben. I'd made it my business to find out what was going on, considering the

153

serious legal ramifications affecting the town. Doctor Barnes also happens to be a good friend of mine, and he'd told me what had happened to Miss King here, and her father. So when the young lady herself turned up with your foreman in the middle of the night, I realized that it was something important, and I invited them in. After she had explained her business, I decided to come back here with her, to await your return.'

'Business? *What* business?' Larry was still puzzled.

With a smile, the girl handed over a folded document. Larry stared at it, and raised his eyebrows.

'This is the notice to quit form I took for the mayor to sign. It was no good when he died, so I brought it back here. . . .'

'Look at again, son.' The judge smiled. 'Miss King brought it with her. You'll see that I've signed it myself. It's legal enough – when there isn't a mayor in office – for a practising judge to do it. As this young lady evidently realized. . . .'

'I read it in Dad's law books,' the girl smiled. 'Remember you suggested I should read them?'

'That was darned clever of you, Val, and I really appreciate it. But perhaps you've had a wasted journey. . . . Listen, I'd better tell you my story now. . . .' And Larry went into the details.

When he had finished, King gave a grim smile. 'I reckon Galt got all he deserved, son. Won't be any need now to serve him notice to quit.'

'If he dies, no,' Larry agreed.

'He'll die,' King said decisively. 'An untreated rattler bite is fatal within a few hours, and it would have taken that before Doc Barnes could get to him – even assuming

154

that puncher you told went to fetch him. Nope, I guess we can wipe Galt off the slate.'

'Not necessarily, Dad,' Val said. 'If he were found in time by that half-breed servant of his, he might have saved him with the old Indian trick.'

'What's that?' Larry asked.

'Cut open the flesh at the point of the bite, suck out the poison, and then cauterize the wound.'

'Never heard of it,' Larry said. 'Can't say I'm sorry either. Anyway, I left Galt to look after himself.'

Judge Gascoigne had been studying the will, whilst listening to Larry's story. He laid it down on the table, alongside a letter he had looked at earlier, given to him by Richard King. It was the letter in which Galt had as good as admitted abducting Val. He adjusted his glasses as Larry and the others looked at him.

'Well, Judge?' Larry said. 'Can you tell me how I stand legally in regard to throwing Galt out of the Double-L and getting him tied up for his various offences?'

'I guess there's nothing to stop you taking over the Double-L and the gold mine any moment you want, son,' he said at length. 'This will is sufficient authority for doing so, allied of course to the valid notice to quit you now have.'

'And his crimes?' Larry asked. 'Assuming, that is, that he's still alive to answer to them.'

'As I said, as the situation stands at present, you can take possession of the ranch and the mine. This 'abduction' letter should be handed over to the Federals in Prescott. They'll have to decide what to do about Galt. You can tell them of his depredations, of course, but without independent witnesses it may be difficult to get a conviction on all of the counts.'

'And in the meantime,' Larry asked, 'do I give Galt time to recover before throwing him out? After all, he's still suffering from the effects of a rattler-bite.'

Judge Gascoigne gave a serious smile. 'Want some advice, son? You kick Galt out here and now. The longer you leave him in peace, the more chance he gets to entrench himself. Considering the enormity of the man's crimes – and that of his associates – there's no longer any room for sentiment.'

'OK,' Larry agreed, picking up the notice to quit. 'I'll deal with him first thing in the morning, after I've ridden into town to get my deputies and some men together in case of any opposition.'

'Before you do that, son,' the judge said, 'you'll need to countersign the form yourself, as sheriff. That entitles you to order Galt to get out – unconditionally. If he doesn't, make sure you have enough men to throw him out.'

'Thanks for the help,' Larry said, adding his signature with the pen King gave him. He glanced up as the girl suddenly gave a tremendous yawn.

'Sorry,' she murmured ruefully.

'If there's any apologizing to be done, it should be by me,' Larry smiled faintly. 'I've kept you all up to this ungodly hour with my talking and questions for the judge. I suggest we all hit the hay immediately, and try to snatch some sleep for what's left of the night.'

'Right,' King agreed. 'Some of the boys are still on the watch, so we can sleep in comfort. I hope.'

Larry helped King to his feet, and Val showed the judge the way to the room she'd prepared for him.

King's hope was fulfilled. Nothing happened in the night, and immediately after breakfast the following morning Larry rode into town. He was accompanied by Judge Gascoigne and Val and her father – who insisted he was well enough to travel – with the girl herself driving the buckboard.

Once the town was reached, Larry lost no time in explaining the circumstances, and then, with his two deputies and a posse of perhaps two dozen men, they all rode out to the Double-L, Larry in the lead.

Rather to his surprise, he found Dr Barnes just upon the point of leaving in his own buckboard. The men of the ranch – the few of them there were about – just stood around, eyeing Larry and his followers narrowly but not daring to attempt anything.

'Been fixing up Galt?' Larry asked the practitioner. 'Looks like you've been working through the night. . . .'

'You're wrong on both counts, son.' Doc Jackson smiled grimly. 'I've spent the night here, true – but I was simply sleeping. I was called out so late, I was too dad-blamed tired to face riding back into town after I'd seen Galt.'

'How *is* Galt?' Larry asked, tight-lipped.

'Take a look for yourself,' the medico said surprisingly. He stood up in the buckboard and pulled aside a large sheet covering the back seat.

Larry gave a start as he looked at the oddly contorted features of Galt.

'He's dead! So you couldn't save him, after all.'

'Wasn't a question of that, son. Galt was stone dead when I got here last night.'

Val had drawn up her own buckboard alongside. She and her passengers had heard the exchange, along with

157

the two leading deputies. They listened intently as Doc Barnes continued his explanation.

'It wasn't the rattler venom that killed Galt, though that certainly contributed. The man actually died of acute heart failure! He was vastly overweight of course, and hardly a fit man. . . .'

'We had a hell of a scrap just before the snake bit him,' Larry said thoughtfully. 'Might that have done it, Doc?'

'It certainly would have put strain on his heart,' the medico conceded. 'But I reckon it was probably sheer fright that did it, as much as anything.' He shrugged. 'The shock killed him. . . .'

Val climbed down from the buckboard and came to Larry's side. 'What now, Larry? You aren't going to ride to the gold mine, are you?' She looked about her, frowning. 'This place seems practically deserted – but some of his men might be holed up at the mine. If so, there'll be danger for you. . . .'

Larry shook his head. 'I don't need to risk that particular confrontation now. Galt and all my enemies are dead. The way is now open for me to take over the Double-L, and the mine can wait a day or two. I'll report everything to the federal authorities in Prescott tomorrow, and let them deal with it. They'll send out a force to clear out the mine for me. Meanwhile. . . .'

He broke off as Judge Gascoigne suddenly got to his feet in the buckboard, and clapped his hands to attract attention. All eyes swung towards him.

'Listen, folks. We need a new mayor to complete the regeneration in Buzzard's Bend. I'm proposing Richard King for the job.' Then he added drily: 'In spite of – or maybe because of – his somewhat unusual legal methods!'

'Sure thing,' agreed several of the posse together.

'Couldn't do better,' said Doc Barnes. 'Mebbe it'll keep him out of trouble, so I can get some sleep at nights!'

King smiled, and waved his good hand in acknowledgement of the general approbation for the suggestion. Then, out of the side of his mouth, as the judge sat back down beside him, he said:

'Say, Judge, what did you mean. by that last remark?'

Gascoigne smiled gravely. 'You know perfectly well. Did you really think I was unaware of your stratagem with the late sheriff's two missing witnesses?'

King looked worried. 'You ain't planning to charge me with anything, are you Judge?'

Gascoigne gave a deep chuckle. 'Why should I? Dame Justice wears a blindfold, doesn't she? What's good enough for her is good enough for me. . . . Wait!' he touched King on the sleeve of his good arm. 'I've been watching your daughter and young Ashfield. I fancy they may have an announcement of their own.'

King swung round to look at his daughter. She and Larry were close together, whispering, her arm resting gently on his shoulder. Larry grinned broadly, and looked up at the two men in the buckboard.

'Week from today it is,' he cried. 'Then the Double-L will get its rightful boss and I'll have the wife I've been waiting for.'